The Ghosts Of
Sky Valley Cozy Mystery
Box Set

William Jarvis

About Us

William Jarvis loves writing mystery stories. Writing is his passion since he was a child. Now, he shares this gift with everyone through his books. He has been writing several book series and aims to do more as he grows more with his writing.

Currently, he is traveling the world while he continues to write where his feet take him.

Get Notice of Our New Releases Here!
http://eepurl.com/7jbzn

Table of Contents

The Deadly Diner

Chapter 1
First Year Blues

The smell of freshly baked eggplant and zucchini lasagna enveloped the kitchen. Emmy Marie Byrne-Lowell put the platter of lasagna down on the table and wiped the sides of it so it won't mess up what she had just set up.

The table looked perfect. There was a floral arrangement of roses and mums as the centerpiece, together with some candles. In the freezer laid some peach-mango pops that she made earlier and there's also a strawberry and cinnamon cake for dessert. It's her and Daniel's first anniversary as a married couple, and she wanted to make this night special amidst all its simplicity.

"Purrrrrrrrrrrr...." Wendy, their seven month old Maine Coon, purled around Emmy's legs which tickled Emmy a bit.

"What is it, girl?" She smiled as she bent down to pet Wendy, not minding that she'd probably get some fur on her red lace dress. Wendy purled some more, then sniffed what's on the table. Emmy laughed. "Oh no, darling girl, those aren't for you," she said, then made her way to open one of the china cabinets in the kitchen. She then took out a can of Wendy's favorite wet food and poured the contents on her bowl where Wendy chomped happily. Emmy couldn't help but smile.

Wendy arrived on their doorstep six months ago. She was so small and so frail. They really didn't know what to do, but they decided to take her in and bring her to the vet. Seven months later and here she is: a strong, a bit bratty, but definitely loving and lovable cat. Somehow, she makes their lives lighter and better.

A lot had changed since the past year or two. For a while, Emmy didn't think that their love would survive because of everything that happened: Annabeth's death, Matthew dying a few days later, Audrina almost being incarcerated, Ruby dying, Frank wreaking havoc on their lives…to say that everything was crazy would be an understatement.

Despite all that, they were able to get through all that and they even got mar ried. It was the happiest day of Emmy's life because she and Daniel really have been through a lot as a couple: the long separation brought upon by her stint in Paris, the fact that she suspected Daniel of having something to do with all the craziness in her life, and how they almost never got together again. She couldn't help but agree that life could hold a lot of surprises with it—and she's happy that with it came Daniel.

When he asked her to marry him at the carnival, a place that meant so much for them, she knew that she wouldn't be able to live with herself if she'd let this opportunity go to waste once more. Besides, their love is a kind of love that's worth fighting for—there was no question about that.

With married life came a lot of adjustments, though. No matter how well they knew each other, Emmy realized that there were still a lot of things you'd know about your partner once you're married. Things such as their sleeping positions, the way they snored—or didn't snore, how they looked like upon waking up in the morning. Then of course, there are other things like how one of you got to annoy the other with the slightest provocations, how voices raise when you fight, how sometimes…you feel like you really do not know each other the way you should.

There's also the fact that Daniel's grandmother, his beloved Nana, died just three months ago. Emmy knew how much this wracked Daniel, but he still stayed strong. She knew how hard it was for him because nana was amazing. She was one of the kindest persons out there, but somehow a stroke just took her away from them.

It wasn't a very easy situation and Emmy thought that Daniel would just shut her out and everything would be ruined. Thankfully Daniel was able to pull through—they were able to pull through.

In the end, the good things overcome the bad and that's what Emmy is happy about. She didn't realize she was just standing there until the doorbell rang and she was jolted back to reality.

"Just a second!" She called out and made her way to the living room, where photos from various points in their relationship lined the walls: the photo they took at that fifth grade recital, a photo Daniel took of hers at their Junior Prom while they were broken up, the moment after they rode the new rollercoaster at the carnival…dinner dates, picnics, and of course, their wedding portrait where they smiled at each other with a lot of love in their eyes.

She then opened the door and was surprised to see a dashing Daniel standing outside the door, a bouquet of roses, wild berries, and lavender in his hand. "Hello, gorgeous lady," he smiled, "Would it be okay if I take you out on a date?"

"Wh—what?" Emmy said then saw that a limousine was also waiting for them. "Dan—"

"What?" he grinned, "Happy anniversary."

"Thank you, but…I cooked for us."

"What?" Daniel then told the limo driver to wait for them for a while then he went inside the house with Emmy where she led him to the dining room. Wendy purred as he saw Daniel and Daniel gave her a pat on the head. "Oh, baby…" He said as he saw what Emmy prepared.

Emmy bit her lip. "What do we do now?" She asked.

"Listen," Daniel said as he placed a hand on her shoulder. "We can still eat this later. I mean, I know you worked hard for this but…I made a reservation for us at this nice restaurant and…I have a surprise for you so…"

"So, we'll just go with your plan then?"

"Em,"

"Fine," she said and took a deep breath. As a planner, she hated it when things go otherwise but then again, at least this was a good thing. At least it's not another death; another murder.

"Okay?"

She nodded her head.

"Come on," he smiled as he held out his hand and he took it. They then made their way out of the house and to the restaurant where a big surprise was waiting for Emmy.

When you're no longer in the world that you used to live in, you realize how different things are; how things are no longer the way they were before, how

13

your bedroom doesn't look the same anymore, how your parents have aged...
how everyone seems to move on without you around.

You realize that no matter how big of an impact you had on them while you
were still around, you can no longer go back to the person you once were;
that you could no longer get back—period, no matter how much you want to.

Then you realize that no matter how much time has passed, even if time no
longer applies to you, there are things that you need to get back to. There are
things that you have to fix, or un-fix.

You have to go back.

You have to be there.

You have to be.

Chapter 2
You're Not The Only One

Emmy couldn't believe her eyes.

As Daniel helped her alight the limo, some people greeted her with bouquets of roses and she was made to walk on a carpeted floor on the way to the door of the restaurant called The Cornerstone, one of the newest restaurants in Sky Valley. It had this old world, rustic charm that could easily captivate anyone. The food was amazing, too.

As the doors of the restaurant opened, Emmy was even more surprised when a group of musicians, some of them playing the violin, started to sing.

You're my light

You're my you

Every day, it's so true

I'll give up anything

Just to be with you

I love you

Make it true

I love you

And it's true

I'm grateful for each day that I have you

Oh, Emmy, I love you

It was a song that she hadn't heard before—a song meant especially for her.

She looked at Daniel and he smiled at her.

"I'm sorry I suck at writing songs…I tried the best that I could but—"

"Are you insane?!" she said and gave him a hug. "That was the best thing anyone ever did for me! I love you, Dan." She then kissed him passionately on the lips, not caring who was watching; it didn't matter—only he did.

He laughed, "Easy, easy." He smiled. "I love you, and you know, you're not the only one who's good with surprises."

She grinned and gave him a peck on the cheeks. "I love you, too."

They then noticed everyone looking at them, some smiling, some whispering, while others were applauding. Emmy bit her lip and smiled.

"Mr. and Mrs. Lowell?" the usherette said and smiled. "May I lead you to your table?"

"Yes, yes of course." Emmy smiled and she and Daniel walked hand in hand to their table at one corner of the restaurant, the view of the fireflies and grass their company. It was romantic; it was special.

Soon, they were able to order some food and so they just relaxed in the company of each other. It was already turning out to be one of the best nights of Emmy's life, until a somewhat 50 year old woman together with her daughter came up to them.

"Hi," the woman said. "Sorry," she smiled, smoothing down her plaid dress. "I really didn't mean to interrupt but…you're Emmy Byrne, right?"

"Emmy Lowell now." Emmy answered and smiled.

"Oh yes, of course." The woman smiled back. "Oh I'm just so happy to see you. I mean, I never see you around and I've always wanted to show my appreciation for what you did…I mean, there's this friend of mine who got incarcerated before and he really wasn't at fault, so that really irked me and his family. I always thought that Lena McMahon was incompetent, but no one really believed me, and when you were able to kick her away from this town…wow, thank you so much." The woman held Emmy's hands. "Thank you, Emmy."

"You're...welcome?" Emmy said unsurely and laughed awkwardly. "Sorry, I mean, it wasn't just me. My husband and my friends helped me out, too. And believe me, Lena was a tough nut to crack."

They all laughed.

"Seriously, thank you," the woman said. "Well then, we have to go. Happy Anniversary!"

"Thanks," Emmy smiled.

But that wasn't even the end of it.

Throughout dinner, Emmy heard people talking about her, saying that she was the woman who changed things at Sky Valley; that McMahon was gone because of her, that if they were in her position, they probably wouldn't be able to survive, and that they probably would've just ran away. All these things already made Emmy feel like going back home, just spending time with Daniel alone and not being around all these brouhaha.

"Em," Daniel reached for her hand. "I'm so sorry," He said. "We can just go home if you want..."

"No, it's okay," Emmy said, thinking that she didn't want to ruin Daniel's plans. "I think I just need to be in the powder room for a bit." she tapped Daniel's hand. "I'll be okay."

She then stood up and made her way to the powder room, hoping that this night wouldn't totally turn into disaster.

There are days when my memory's already hazy; when I could no longer remember how everything happened, or why they happened. That's why I am trying so hard to stay...to be here. To get back on those who ruined me; to get back to those who made me this way.

I want to plot out my revenge. Actually, I already have. It's taken a lot from me, though. It's taken my hope to finally be at peace, the last few shards of my strength—or whatever it is that's keeping me here.

But you know what I haven't lost?

My faith.

My faith in the fact that I would get the justice that has long been taken from me.

I'll get it back.

I'll be back.

Chapter 3
The Engagement

Emmy just arrived inside the powder room when a brunette woman bumped into her and spilled a little something on her dress—and Emmy wasn't sure what it was. She only saw that it came inside the woman's intricately designed small hip flask, smaller than the usual ones you see in the market.

"Oh gosh!" The woman said. Emmy recognized her as the woman from one of the other tables near them. "Oh my goodness, I'm sorry," the woman said as she took a handkerchief from her purse and wiped Emmy's lace dress with it. Emmy noticed that the woman was trembling. She looked extremely nervous and even shady.

"It's okay," Emmy said. "I'm fine. It's nothing."

"No...it's..." The woman sighed. Emmy looked at her and noticed that she was actually beautiful: her brunette locks were shiny, her hazel eyes spoke volumes and she would actually look confident if only she wasn't so frazzled. Was she frazzled because she spilled that thing on Emmy? It really wasn't such a big deal, Emmy thought.

"I'm really sorry, I wasn't looking."

"It's okay," Emmy said and smiled. "Look, it's not even showing." She laughed.

The woman smiled back nervously. "Uhm...I should go," she said, "Sorry again." Emmy watched as the woman made her way out of the powder room. She then went inside the cubicles, peed and fixed herself, then checked her reflection on the mirror as she washed her hands.

I'm not going to let those other people ruin this night, she told herself. It's okay. She smiled at herself in the mirror, took a deep breath, and made her way out.

"Okay now?" Daniel asked as he helped Emmy sit down.

"Of course," she smiled at him.

Just then, the musicians started playing again, but not for them. Instead, they positioned themselves near the table of the brunette woman who spilled her drink on Emmy. The woman was sitting with another brunette woman, whose hair was cut just above the shoulders and wearing a white lace dress. She looked absolutely divine, and even if Emmy didn't know her, she thought that the woman seemed kind; like she would do nothing wrong.

But then again, she could be wrong.

Next to the ladies was a man whom Emmy wasn't familiar with. He's probably one of those people who started living in Sky Valley the time that Emmy moved to Paris—or maybe, she really just didn't know him at all. He looked pretty decent and nice with his faux hawk, a button-down shirt and jeans. He looked pretty nervous, too, but Emmy thought that it was the good kind of nervous, instead of the one she saw at the Brunette woman earlier.

Emmy, Daniel and the rest of the people watched as the musicians played their own version of Oliver James' The Greatest Story Ever Told and then suddenly, the man in their table stood up and faced the woman in white.

"Tyler—what—" the woman said. She then looked at the other woman, "Bree? Do you—"

The woman named Bree shrugged, but still looked nervous. She was holding onto her hip flask.

Tyler grinned and started to speak, "Tonight feels like a celebration of love, huh?" He laughed. "Anyway..." It was so obvious that he was nervous, but he went on and said, "Angeline," he held one of the woman's hands, "it's been a while since we became a couple...sometimes, I think you feel like I don't love you the way you want to be loved but...but I want you to know that I love you with all that I have and with all that I am. I love you because...because you deserve to be loved. You're a great person, Angeline. You're kinder than anyone your age, than anyone, period. You're amazing, and smart, and interesting and...and I don't know what I'd do without you. I could no longer imagine me without you. I know that sounds tacky but..." He sighed, "We have been through a lot over the years and I know, deep down, I probably wouldn't have survived without you around. So, Angeline," he went down on one knee, "I'm asking you now...will you marry me?"

"Tyler…" Angeline already had tears in her eyes.

"Yes?"

Angeline nodded and knelt down to hug Tyler. "Yes," she said. "Yes, I'll marry you!"

Tyler and Angeline laughed amidst the tears. They hugged each other and stayed in their bubble for what seemed like a moment, grateful for the applause and cheers from the crowd.

"That's sweet, isn't it?" Emmy smiled at Daniel.

"Definitely," Daniel smiled as he reached for her hand.

"But she looks sad." Emmy said, noticing how the other brunette woman was holding onto her hip flask a little tighter than usual, her face in shock, and her eyes brimming with sadness. That's the thing about sadness, Emmy thought, it shows itself even in the happiest of situations; you couldn't deny that it's real.

"Who?"

"Her," Emmy pursed her lips towards Bree. "I actually bumped into her at the powder room, she spilled her drink on my dress and she just looked so nervous." She took a deep breath, "I feel like her nervousness has a lot to do with their engagement. Like, maybe, she's not ready for it because I don't know… maybe she likes the guy. Or she's protective of the girl." She sighed, "I really shouldn't be thinking about this, huh?"

They both laughed and thanked the maitre'd for sending them their orders: lamb chops, a scallop and shrimp bowl, and mango-lychee and strawberry-mandarin cakes. The wine was divine, too—like Daniel chose it especially for this occasion.

"You know," Daniel said. "Sometimes, I feel like I wasn't able to give you a proper proposal. Like, there's more that I could've done."

Emmy laughed. "Nonsense," She said. "I'm glad for how things turned out between us, for us, and…" She squeezed Daniel's hand. "I'm glad because I'm with you." She smiled. "Now, should we eat or what?"

They laughed and started working on their meals.

I used to believe in love.

I used to believe that when you like someone, the universe will work in such a way that it will be good for you both; that things will work out between you two.

I was so young when I first realized that I liked him. I was so young when I thought that I could be with him, that we'd go to the prom together, that maybe when we graduate from High School, we could leave this town and we could start over, just the two of us.

But she ruined everything.

Or maybe, he did.

Maybe, he just never saw me as someone he could be together with. Maybe, I was too plain. Maybe, I just wasn't his type.

But somehow, it didn't feel that way. Somehow, when you kissed me that afternoon, I knew that you also had feelings for me. I knew that the way you looked at me had a lot to do with how you really saw me; I knew you wanted it to be something bigger than it was.

That's what you said, right?

You told me you'll end it with her, and we'd be good and blah blah blah.

PROMISES.

Promises could kill.

I was so young when I first fell for you.

And now...I'm still young, but everything about me feels old.

Chapter 4
Scream For Your Life

"It's so funny how she wants to actually put fireplaces in almost every part of the house," Daniel said. He was telling Emmy a story about one of his clients, one Elizabeth Grant who apparently was obsessed with installing fireplaces in her house. Daniel was now back to his architectural roots, practicing what he studied once again. He stopped for a while to take on freelancing jobs, but he decided to go back to work after they got married so he'd be able to provide more for her—and for their future. "Talk about a crazy kind of obsession!"

Emmy laughed as she took a bite of the mango-lychee cake. "Aren't all obsessions crazy?" she asked. "I mean, when you think about it, Lena was pretty obsessed about dad so that led her to do all those things. And then Annabeth was so crazy about being the perfect daughter and all that so she forgot that her feelings were actually real and valid. She forgot that she had the right to choose her own path, instead of just living up to everyone's expectations, you know what I mean?"

"Yeah," Daniel said. "I guess you could say that things are never really in black and white, at least not most of the time."

"You could say that," Emmy said. "Audrina called, by the way."

"Yeah? How is she?"

"She's good," Emmy smiled. "You know, I feel like an engagement is coming for her and dad soon."

"Yeah?" Daniel asked. "And how'd you feel about that?"

"You know what?" She said. "It's fine. I mean it's awkward, of course, but she's in the right age and dad's smitten with her. She makes him happy. When I left, dad was so devastated and…and I thought I'd never see him happy again. He loved mom, and mom will always be my mother but…I wouldn't stand in the way of their happiness. Audrina's amazing."

"She is," Daniel said. "If I were her, I probably wouldn't have forgiven us when we accused her of—"

"I know," Emmy took a deep breath. "Oh well, at least we all have moved on from that."

"And Tripp and Lena are both incarcerated."

"They're insane, both of them," Emmy said. "I couldn't believe they were able to do all that. And Selena's still keen on putting me down, even setting up this hate page for me."

"Some people at work talk about that, you know," he said. "But don't worry, honey, you have more fans than haters."

"Fans, huh?"

"You're a star," he said, "and quite frankly, you cook better than the people here."

"See? I told you," she teased. "But then again…your surprise was amazing. I think you deserve a gift tonight."

He grinned, "Really? Should I dress up for it? Or maybe, dress down—"

She tapped him gently on the arm. "Shut. Up," She said.

They continued eating and chatting and were still having some fun when suddenly, everyone were disrupted by the shrill screams of someone from the powder room, her screams a knife cutting the silence down.

"AAHHHHHHH!!!! NOOOOOOOOOOOOOO!!!!!"

Death is a funny thing.

You know how when you're a kid, you thought that you'd be so scared of death and that it'll only happen when you're old and lanky and wrinkly… but alas, death could come knocking on your door any time, any day!

Sometimes, I wonder how things would've turned out if I stayed alive; if I didn't go out of this world the way I did. Sometimes, I wonder how it would have been like if the person who killed me was caught.

Of course, that wouldn't bring me back to life, but still…

I remember events from that day.

I remember almost everything but when it comes to my death…it's painful.

You think death ends pain?

Think again.

How can I not be in pain when it's been years and my killer is still out there, celebrating?

You know what I remember the most, though?

I remember confusion. I remember the feel of water on my skin, the smell of that place…

And mostly, I remember betrayal.

I remember betrayal more than anything else.

I remember how I trusted her; how I trusted them, and what did I ever get from that?

Nothing.

Nothing but death.

Chapter 5
Goodbye Angeline

"AHHHHHH!!!!" The woman's screams were still so loud that a few people were prompted to check what was happening. The maitre'd asked everyone to stay in their seats, but of course, some people couldn't just sit down after hearing all those things.

The manager of the restaurant made her way to the powder room, and when the door was opened everyone gasped and were left in shock to see Angeline, the woman who just got engaged earlier, lying down on the floor. She appeared lifeless.

"Angie!" Her fiancé, Tyler screamed, "Oh no, Angie!" He then pushed through the swarming crowd and hastily made his way towards the body of his fiancé. He shook her. "Angie! What happened?! Call the doctor, please! Call the police!" He was panicking now and everyone else was on their toes, too.

Bree, who apparently was Angeline's sister, was also sitting down on the floor, hugging herself. She was crying and shaking.

"What happened?!" Tyler asked her. "Bree, what happened?!"

"I don't know!" Bree spat at him. "How will I know? I was inside one of those cubicles and when I got out, I found her like that. She was…she's on the floor, her mouth bubbling. I…I have no idea how this could have happened. Oh my god. That's my sister!" She cried, buckets of tears flowing out of her eyes. "Please…please help us."

"Everyone, please go home," The manager said. "I am so sorry for this inconvenience—"

"Inconvenience?!" Tyler shouted. "My fiancée's—"

"We just called 911 and the police—"

"Everyone please go home."

People slowly but hesitantly made their way out of the restaurant, talking about how things could have been that way and how everything was so peaceful earlier. Even Emmy was shook up; she didn't know how to react.

As they made their way to the limo, they bumped into the woman who spoke to them earlier, the one who said she was thankful that Lena McMahon was gone. "Oh," she said as she saw Daniel and Emmy, "sorry…that was…that was quite unfortunate."

Emmy nodded, "Looks like the troubles in Sky Valley are starting again."

"Calm down, child," the woman said. "We still don't know what this is. "Anyway, we have to go. Do take care of yourselves."

Emmy nodded and let Dan open the car door for her. She couldn't wait to go home.

Old habits die hard, they say.

And you know what? I believe them.

When you know that a person is capable of betraying her closest friend, you do know that she can betray her sister, too. Sometimes, blood is not thicker than water.

People have all these things that they want. People have other people that they want, so of course, they do have the tendency to hurt whoever gets in their way. I do understand the motive. What I don't understand is how she could do it.

Oh no, just because I'm a ghost doesn't mean I have no idea what I'm saying. I'm not entirely sure, but it's palpable. It's not impossible that she's the one who hurt me before, and it's not impossible that she's the one who hurt Angeline, too.

She's still her old evil self.

I know. I had to prove it.

And what she did today?

That justifies that she's really the reason why I could no longer live on this earth.

But don't worry, Bree, the cops will get you—and you'll rot in prison hell forever.

Chapter 6
Ghosts Of Murders Past

"What I don't understand," Emmy said as she put the comforter over the bed and smoothed it down, "is how that could have happened. The news says that it's probably just food poisoning, but come on, Dan." she said, the TV blaring news about Angeline's death in the background.

What the police knew, as of now, is that Angeline died due to food poisoning, and more investigations will be done. Both Tyler and Bree were taken in for questioning.

"If she died because of food poisoning then shouldn't it be imperative that we'll all be poisoned, too, especially if the poison is strong enough to kill someone?" Emmy asked.

"Yeah, I was thinking about that, too." Daniel said. "It's like someone did this especially for her, to hurt her."

"And why would anyone do that? She looks so nice…so fragile. And she just got engaged, for heaven's sake! It's just so unfair."

"Honey, nothing's ever fair," Dan patted Emmy on the arm.

"I know, but…" she took a deep breath. "You know, I feel like that Bree girl has something to do with this."

"Because she was at the crime scene?"

"Because of the look in her eyes when they got engaged. She's hurt, Dan, I could totally tell. That's not the look of someone who's happy for her sister or for her friends, especially on an occasion like that. She wasn't exactly celebrating. And she was so weird when I saw her at the powder room, like she was hiding something. Like—"

"Relax," Daniel told her as he kissed her on the lips. "You need to stop worrying. This isn't our problem anymore."

"But Dan—"

"I know it's hard, especially since we were there, but honey…you have to learn to let go of some things. Not everything is under our control."

"I know," she said, "but it just seems unfair."

He kissed her on the forehead then trailed his way down to her lips. "I love you," he told her, "It's our anniversary, Em, you have to relax."

She looked in his eyes and laughed. He was right, she thought, it's their anniversary, after all. And yet, she couldn't stop thinking about what happened, when in fact they really had nothing to do with it. Everything was just coincidence—or was it?

Enough thinking, Emmy told herself. She then gave in and kissed Daniel passionately on the lips. Soon enough, clothes were being thrown off the floor, and they no longer cared about the world outside; only focusing on each other, wrapping themselves in sheets of flannel, making love and making dreams.

When they were finished, both of them satisfied, Daniel looked at her and gave her a kiss on the forehead. "I love you," He said.

"I love you, too."

"You know," he said, holding her hand, "sometimes, I still can't believe that we're married."

"Like you want to get divorced?"

"What? No!" He laughed, "Where'd you get that idea? What I mean is… sometimes, all of this still seem surreal. Like, sometimes, you just look back on everything and you wonder how on earth you got to where you are right now. But with us, it's a good thing. It's always a good thing."

"Even though we've been through a lot?" she asked.

"Those things don't matter anymore."

They kissed and she spoke, "I kind of feel…scared."

"Because of what happened to Angeline? Yeah, me too, but you know…this isn't about us anymore. It'll be okay. We'll be okay. We'll get through this."

***

Emmy rolled over in her sleep. Somehow she felt so cold, even though Daniel was hugging her. She didn't know why she felt so cold when the weather was pretty humid earlier, and she's not really the type of person who gets cold easily. She tossed and turned, but Daniel still wouldn't budge and he was snoring.

She then decided to get up and have a hot cup of tea. She was still so sleepy, but she thought that she really wouldn't be able to sleep feeling the way she does—like she was ice cold and freezing!

And then she realized that it wasn't her who felt ice cold—it was the room. This shocked her because as she set her foot down on the floor, she noticed that it was as if she was walking on ice. She felt so lost and confused. What was happening?

"Dan," She said, trying to wake up Dan. She then took her monogrammed silk robe from one of the chairs on the dresser and put it on. It almost did nothing; she still felt so cold and sick.

She was about to get out of the room when she felt like someone was looking at her and calling her from the outside. She turned towards the window and got the shock of her life—there outside was a woman in white. Her face was so pale, her hair being blown by the wind.

She didn't know if she still believed in ghosts, but that woman was the closest she ever saw to what a ghost would look like.

"Emmy," The woman said. "Emmy, talk to me." Her voice seemed hollow. She seemed hollow.

"Who—who are you—" Emmy muttered.

"Emmy—"

"You're not real, right? I'm just dreaming. This is just a dream and—"

"Of course, I'm real," the woman said. "How do you think the floor would be

33

that cold if I wasn't around?"

"AHHHHHHHHHHHHHH!!!!!" Emmy couldn't help but scream.

It's a funny thing, showing yourself to people.

Most of you think that it's so easy for us; that we show ourselves to you to scare you, but what would be the point in that?

I have to admit, I did do it on purpose before...maybe twice, or thrice. I don't know anymore.

The first few times, I just wanted to scare people because they kept talking about the dead; how they want to see ghosts, how some of them didn't believe in ghosts, yada, yada. And then, when you show yourself to them, they get so scared they run away.

Sometimes people could be funny. Most times, they aren't.

Today though, I wanted to show myself to Emmy because I want her to figure out what happened to Angeline, even though I already have an idea about what happened. But I want to be sure.

What have I got to do with this?

A lot, you know. But I'll tell you about all of that later.

For now, I have to figure out how to talk to Emmy again without scaring her.

She's considered the resident sleuth but she's scared of ghosts?

Damn, my life is screwed.

Oh, wait.

I actually don't have a life anymore.

Chapter 7
Where Are You?

"AHHHHHHH!!!!!"

Emmy's screams woke Daniel up from his slumber. He was surprised to see her slumped down on the floor, screaming like she just saw a ghost.

"Em?" he said and hastily got out of bed to check out what was happening. He then wrapped his arms around Emmy. "What's going on? Who's there? What happened?"

"A g-ghost," She stammered.

"What?"

She looked at him with fear and confusion in her eyes. "There's a ghost," she said and pointed out the window, "right there. There's this woman in white and she looked…she looked dead. It's a ghost, Dan! She was just there and—"
"What?" Daniel asked, confused. He never knew that Emmy had this thing about ghosts and stuff. "Calm down—"

"No! We have to look for her!" she said, stood up and hastily made her way out of the room, Daniel trailing close behind.

First, Emmy checked out the back door and Daniel went out the front door. Then they both checked the living room and the kitchen. In the kitchen, their cat Wendy started meowing. She was meowing so loud, Emmy thought that maybe she could sense the ghost too.

"What is it, Wends?" She asked. "You can sense her too, right? She's here, right? Where is she?"

"Honey, no one's here," Daniel said.

"But that's impossible, because I just saw her, and look at Wendy!"

"She's probably just hungry," Daniel said. He then opened the cabinet and took out some wet food for Wendy to munch on. The cat happily ate, "See?" Emmy sighed, "But I saw her."

Daniel gave her a glass of water. Emmy drank some but she still couldn't help but think of the woman she saw. *Why did she see her? What was she doing in their house? What does she want?*

"Are you sure that it's not a real person? Maybe we should just call the police—"

"Dan, I know what a real person looks like. She's definitely not like us."

"Maybe you're just stressed out. Maybe, what you saw was nana—"

"It wasn't nana, Dan," she said. "I would know nana anywhere. She's…different. She looked so weird, so frazzled, her face so pale…I don't know who she is or what she's doing here."

"Relax," Daniel said and massaged Emmy on the shoulders. "But…it's your first time seeing a ghost, right? Maybe, it was just a product of being tired and restless and because of everything that happened this evening—"

"Dan," she sighed. "I know what I saw, okay? And…it's really not my first encounter with something like that."

"What?" Daniel asked, confused, as he heated the eggplant lasagna that Emmy made earlier. Emmy never told him anything about ghosts before.

Emmy took a deep breath. She stood up, drank some water, and petted Wendy before looking out the window, stirring up old memories inside her. "You know," he said, "I'm not this big believer of ghosts but when…when my mother died, you know how that affected me, right?" She looked at Dan. "It wasn't the easiest of times. There were nights when I would just go and talk to her; even wanting her to answer me back just so I'd know that she was still around. Anyway, one night I decided to spend some time in her study…you know that place; we used to play around there when we were kids." She and Dan shared a smile as Dan was now plating the lasagna.

"Anyway…that night I just wanted to spend some time there, maybe just so I'd be filled with her memory, you know what I mean? Then, surprise! I saw this woman sitting on her chair, looking out the window. The thing is…I knew it wasn't a real woman. I'd know a real woman, a real person, anywhere. For a couple of seconds, I just stood there not knowing what to do, and then I decided to check out who it was and voila! She disappeared just like that.

"I didn't really know how to feel but somehow, I felt betrayed… because, you know, I hoped that I could talk to my mom. I wished that we could catch up, just be together again…even for just a few seconds, but I don't know…I guess, she just wanted me to know that she's okay, if that even makes sense." She sighed, "I don't know, Dan, but I think the woman I saw earlier…no, she's not even a woman, she seemed like a girl… like she was in her teens or something. And she looked sad and harassed and…it felt like she wanted to tell me something. She even called my name, you know? She knows me. There's a reason why she's here and that's why I want to find her."

Daniel took a deep breath after eating some lasagna. He drank some water and spoke. "You know, I kind of wish I could see nana, too," he said, "but I guess it's also okay that she's not showing herself because maybe, that's a sign that she's at peace."

"But the girl—"

"I know it's bothering you. It could really bother anyone, you know? But I guess… you just have to let it go for now."

"But what if I could help her?" She asked. "What if…what if the reason why she showed herself to me was because there's something I could help her with?"

"But you said you don't know her, so how could she ask help from you if you guys don't know each other?"

"I don't know, Dan," she said, "I'm not a ghost expert. Maybe I should just see a medium or a ghost communicator or whatever."

"Hey, hey," he said and reached for her hand. "Look, tonight's been eventful, but maybe we should just let it go, okay?" He said, "It's late, we have work tomorrow—"

"Fine," she cut him off. "Fine, I'll just…let me wash the dishes."

"The dishes can wait."

"No, I want to."

He took a deep breath, stood up, and gave her a kiss on the forehead. "Okay, but don't take too long, okay? It's late."

She smiled meekly and nodded. "Okay," she said and watched Daniel walk back to their room. She took Wendy from the floor and let her sit on her lap. Wendy purred as Emmy petted her, thinking about ghosts of the past and how she could move forward this way.

It's never easy finding who your target could be.

Okay, okay, that sounded wrong. I chose to show myself to Emmy because I know she could help me...but I have to find a way to show myself to her again without scaring her. Her husband doesn't believe in me, anyway, or he refuses to believe in me.

I can't blame him. I mean, you really can never expect everyone to see you when you're a ghost, just like you can't expect everyone to see you and look at you when you're still alive.

All my life (excuse the pun) I've been invisible to a lot of people. I was the kind of girl who wasn't pretty enough, who wasn't popular enough...who wasn't this and that. You know what I mean?

And now I have to use all my might just to make someone see me so she could help me.

I may not be alive anymore—but it doesn't mean that I no longer have a place in this world.

Everyone will soon know that.

I'll make sure of it.

Chapter 8
You've Got To Help Me

Daniel went to work early the following morning so Emmy decided that she'd just clean up the house. Cleaning the house is one of those things that keep her sane, especially in times like this.

She fed Wendy her favorite cat food, wiped the shelves, and went on mopping the house. She also spent some time fixing the bed and organizing the books in an alphabetized manner. Those books kept her company, especially in times when she feels alone in the house. They take her to places she's never been to before.

She also took a hot shower and fixed herself so she could calm down. Last night's events were still embedded in her mind. At half past ten the doorbell rang and she was surprised, because she knew that Daniel was at work and no one sent her a message about visiting her today. She took one last look at herself in the mirror then went down the stairs and opened the main door.

Emmy was all the more surprised when she saw Bree, Angeline's sister and the woman who bumped into her last night, standing outside the door. Her hair was in a ponytail, wearing a sunflower printed cap-sleeved dress and looking every bit as frazzled as she could be.

"Bree, right?" Emmy asked, "What are you doing here?"

"Can we talk?"

Emmy was confused. She knew she had nothing to do with Bree or Angeline or any of the events of the past evening. She took a deep breath. "Come in," she said, the hesitation evident in her voice. "Let me just get some drinks…" She then went to the kitchen to make some fruit juice for her and Bree, contemplating whether she could call Daniel and let him know about this or not. She then decided that she shouldn't, because she didn't want him to get worried and in a way, she also wanted to know what Bree was doing in her place. She then got out of the kitchen seconds later, a tray of fruit juice and strawberry filled cookies in her hands. She handed Bree a glass and poured some juice in. "Feel free to eat," she said.

"Thanks." Bree said.

Emmy watched Bree drink some juice. Somehow she looked frail; like she was only trying to be strong for today. Emmy wondered some more about what Bree was doing there when she could just spend time at her sister's wake—or something close to that.

"So…" Emmy said after drinking some juice herself. "May I ask what you're doing here?"

Bree looked at her for a couple of seconds and didn't say anything.

"Bree?"

Bree took a deep breath. "Sorry, I was just…" she sighed. "I need your help."

"My… help?"

"Look," Bree said, "I know what you've done for this town. Heck, everyone does. And…and I thought, maybe you could help me figure out what happened to my sister."

"Wasn't it just food poisoning?"

"Yeah, that's what the authorities are saying," Bree answered, "but…but what if there's something more?"

"What do you mean something more?" Emmy asked.

"I don't know." Bree said and sighed, "Like maybe…maybe, Tyler did this?"

"What?!" Emmy asked, surprised. Where was all this coming from and why would Bree think that she could help her with this? "Look, I really have no idea what you're doing here, but I think its best that you go home. Spend time with your sister for the last few days; spend time with your family—"

"But you helped other people before, right? Or do you just help people when you know your life is at stake?" she asked. "Remember when your friend was killed and you did all that you could to figure out what happened? Or when you had that tryst with Frank Holt and you figured out that he was actually married? Or—"

"Enough," Emmy stated. She really didn't want to look back to that point in her life anymore. "What is this about, anyway?" she asked. "I mean, if you need help, why don't you ask the police?"

"You know how incompetent they could be," she said. "You see how they decide that the first conclusion they come to is the reason why things happen. They fail to actually study the case, or have you forgotten how Lena McMahon played you and made you feel so stupid and betrayed you?"

"I said, enough about that," Emmy repeated. "Look, Bree, I'm really sorry about what happened to your sister. She looked really nice—"

"Everyone says that. She's like, everyone's favorite," she rolled her eyes.

"And you don't really like that?"

"I wouldn't ask you for help if I didn't like that or if I hated my sister."

"Right," Emmy muttered, not sure if she should actually believe Bree.

"Please," Bree said and reached for Emmy's hand. Bree's hands were cold and shaking. "Please, you've got to help me. You have to help me prove that Tyler has something to do with this."

"And why would I do that?" Emmy asked. "I don't even know him. It would be unfair for me to do this when I don't even know him."

"You have to help me," Bree said, "because I'm telling the truth."

For a while, Emmy didn't know what to say. She thought about Annabeth and Matthew. She thought about how Ruby's hatred made her do the things she did; how Ruby was prompted to kill her own husband…how everything went downhill because of Lena McMahon and Tripp Meyer.

She wanted nothing to do with this, but here was Bree—someone she didn't know. She was just someone she just had a brush with last night, asking her for help.

41

Emmy wasn't a saint, but she always believed that if you could help people, then you should do so. She didn't know what was going on, she didn't know how things would go on, but she couldn't just let this go.

She looked Bree in the eyes and spoke, "I'll see what I can do."

People could always surprise you; sometimes though, you're no longer sure if you could still be surprised or what.

Bree had always been tough as a kid.

I heard that when she was still in California, and some people taunted her for her Latina roots (her mother's Part-Mexican), she talked to those bullies in fluent Spanish and told them off.

I heard that when her mother was hesitant about moving to Sky Valley, back when she was 12, she told her mother that she could fly alone. She wasn't scared—she'll be okay.

When she first showed up in our house after years of being in California, you could see that she never really felt awkward or shy—it was as if she knew that she could command anyone with her presence, and that there's no reason for her to feel small or different from anyone else.

That's Bree, you know? What she wants, she gets. What she doesn't want, she kicks away. That's always been her pattern—and that will always be her pattern.

How can I be so sure?

I just know, okay?

I just know.

Chapter 9
I Think I Know Who Did This

"So, how are you? You okay?" Daniel asked Emmy from the other end of the line. He called to check up on her.

"I'm good," Emmy said. "Wendy misses you." She teased as Wendy purled on her legs.

"Aww, tell the sweet kitty I'll be home early tonight."

"That's awesome," Emmy smiled. "And hey, uh…I have something to tell you…"

"What is it?"

"I'll just tell you later, okay?" She said and heard the doorbell ringing. "Someone's outside. I'll see you later, okay?"

"Alright," Daniel said. "I love you."

"I love you, too."

Emmy then made her way to the front door to see who was outside and got another shock when she saw Tyler, Angeline's fiancé, outside the door.

"Oh good lord," Emmy muttered, "you."

"Hi," Tyler said meekly. "Can I come in?"

"Please," Emmy said, though she didn't really mean it. Why is this house becoming an investigation office? She thought. It's just so weird. "Can I get you anything?" She asked.

"Oh no, please, I just…I just wanted to talk to you." He said.

"Shouldn't you be at your fiancée's wake?"

"Yeah, but I need to ask you for help," he said. "Sorry I came up just like this…I just didn't know what else to do. I thought I'd just see you, and look for your house because of you know…what you've already done for this town in the past. I thought you'd be the perfect person to help me—"

"Why do you think that I could help you? I don't even know you. Except for last night, we haven't spent time together before. And…this really isn't my job."

"I know," he answered. "I'm just…I'm just taking my chances." He took a deep breath, "I just thought maybe, you could help shed light on this…on Angeline's death. I know the police already ruled it as food poisoning but I don't think it's as simple as that. There's always something deeper than reasons on the surface, right?"

She bit her lip. "I get what you're saying," she said, "but, Tyler, this is way beyond my control."

"I know," he said, "but I just thought you'd understand." He went on. "I…I think I know who did this."

Emmy was confused. "You think you know who did this?" She asked. "Who do you think, then?"

"Bree," he answered. "She's the only one who could do this, who would do this."

"What?" She asked, "Why would you say that? Angeline's her sister."

"You know that blood isn't always thicker than water," he told Emmy. "You know how crazy some people get when… when they have ulterior motives."

"Ulterior motives? What do you mean?"

"Look," he said. "I've known Bree all these years, okay? She and I have been friends, together with Angeline and some other girls and…and things haven't always been a bed of roses for any of us. And… there were some traumatic stuff that happened in the past and maybe, maybe, Bree's still not over those things. I've always suspected that—" He stopped suddenly, "Never mind."

"That what?"

44

"No, just, ignore I said that," he said. "The point is that Bree has a lot of motive to do this. I don't want to think ill of her because you know…she's Angeline's sister, and she has also been a good friend to me, to all of us…but, I don't know. We could all be pushed towards the edge sometimes."

"But that's a grave accusation."

"I know," he said, "but I guess she'd say the same thing about me, if she ever talks to you."

Emmy took a deep breath.

Tyler went on. "I just…I just hope you know that I did love Angeline. Maybe, I wasn't the best boyfriend. Maybe, things are still tainted by what happened before, but I loved her with all that I could. I don't have all the riches in the world and…sometimes I still think about things that people shouldn't think of anymore but…but I loved her. I want to seek justice for her. Please," he was about to cry but pulled back and took a business card from his shirt pocket and handed it to Emmy, "Please call me." He then stood up and made his way out of the house.

Emmy stood up too and didn't know how to feel. It was definitely one of the craziest days of her life and was made all the more crazy by the loud growls coming from Wendy in the kitchen.

"What is it, Wendy?"

Emmy didn't know that, once more, she was in for the shock of her life.

Love and hate are on two ends of the spectrum but are similar in such a way that they could make you do things you never thought you'd be able to do in your life.

Tyler?

Well, you could say he was the one great love of my young life but now, I feel like he doesn't actually deserve it.

He hurt me, humiliated me and betrayed me like that.

Somehow, he's at fault, too.

And...sometimes I feel like he knows more than he lets on.

Whatever.

You know, I also feel like, at some point, I'm also glad that Angeline's gone now because at least I wouldn't feel like you just used her; or maybe you just used me.

Ah, don't mind me. You'll know everything soon.

I'll know everything soon.

And go on, sweet little Wendy, growl and hiss until your beloved Emmy sees me.

Chapter 10
Enter Lucy

"Groooooowwwwwwlllllllll ssssssssss" Those were just some of the sounds Emmy heard come from Wendy in the kitchen that made her make her way there fast. "Wendy? What—"

But before she could even finish what she wanted to say, she was taken aback when she saw the ghost of the woman she just saw last night. Emmy couldn't believe her eyes.

"You."

"Hi, Emmy," the ghost said. She sounded calmer now, although her face still looked frail, no matter how young she seemed.

"Oh my goodness," Emmy said. She felt like she was going to faint. "Please tell me this isn't true."

"Please don't faint," The specter said. "I'm harmless." She then swooped around Emmy and touched her. "See? I couldn't touch you the way you think I could." She smiled and twirled in her cap-sleeved white dress, "I'm Lucy, by the way."

"Oh no, please go away."

"Emmy, please, I am not going to hurt you. I just want to talk to you. I need your help."

"Oh god, why do all of you think you can ask me for help?" Emmy asked. "What do I have to do with you?"

"Nothing and everything," Lucy replied and laughed. "Okay, I'm scaring you, aren't I?"

"You're a ghost, how can I not be scared?"

"But you're really not scared. You just think that you are."

"Enough already," Emmy said. "What in god's name do you think you're doing? Why don't you just tell me what you want?"

"I already told you, Emmy," Lucy said, "I need your help." She came near Emmy and spoke again, leaving Emmy feeling as cold and creepy as can be, "You see, I've been observing you from afar for so long. Somehow, I admire you for doing what you did for Sky Valley. That's why I decided that I have to talk to you. I know you'd be able to help me."

"Help you with what?" Emmy said. "Excuse me but you're dead and I have no idea how I could—"

"Shut up," Lucy said. "I know I'm dead. Do you think I don't know my situation? I'm asking you for help because I know what you can do. I know you could help me get Bree in jail. You're still alive. You can do it."

"Wait, what?" Emmy asked. "Why do you want me to put Bree in jail? Do you know her?"

"Do I know her? Ha!" Lucy scoffed. "That girl is my cousin, and so is Angeline. I want Bree in jail because she's…insane, and evil. She's the kind of girl who's rotten to the core and I don't want her anywhere. She killed Angeline, like she killed me all those years ago."

"What?" Emmy asked. "Look, if she killed you, then why is she out there?"

"Because the police are stupid, duh. They ruled out my death as an accident just because they didn't have enough evidence, just like they're doing with Angeline now. You see how easily they ruled out her death as food poisoning? They're being stupid. They don't know that the killer is just working under their noses, and she was even here earlier, right?"

"If you saw her then why didn't you just show yourself to her?"

"Because it's not that easy!" Lucy said. "And she already chose to bury me in her subconscious, you know what I mean? But well, she could hear me… and hear me she did."

Emmy was confused, "What does that even mean?"

"It means what it means," Lucy answered. "Emmy, Bree needs to be in jail; if not for me, than at least for Angeline. At least one of us deserves some justice, you know? Bree doesn't deserve to be out there."

"But she told me—"

"Forget about whatever she told you because between her and Tyler. It's Tyler you should trust. Not that he's very trustworthy and all that but…" she sighed, her sighs hollow and unordinary, "I know him, okay? I know both of them. Just remember how Bree reacted when Angeline and Tyler got engaged. She wasn't exactly happy, right? Do you remember what she was holding?"

"The hip flask?"

"What did you notice about it?"

"I don't know…that it's smaller than any ordinary hip flask and she seemed so nervous when she spilled some on me."

"Right," Lucy said. "It's because she poisoned that hip flask and let Angeline drink the contents when they went to the powder room right after Angeline and Tyler got engaged."

"And you know all these because…?"

"Because I could see everything," Lucy said abruptly.

"And what would Bree's motive be?"

Lucy sighed. "I thought you were smarter than that!" she said. "She likes Tyler, of course. She always had feelings for him and that's why she killed me years ago. I was drowned in water, you know."

"Water? Water where?"

"I don't know…the bathroom—" Lucy went on, "Enough about me," she said. "It's Bree you have to focus on now. It's so hard for me to show myself to you, especially because you don't know me, so don't you dare let this go to waste. You need to help me, Emmy. You need to show all these people that sometimes, truth is stranger and far more different than it seems."

"But—"

But before Emmy could say another word, the doorbell rang and when she looked at where Lucy was just seconds ago, she was no longer there.

One thing I find funny about most people is that they never believe what they should believe in, but they believe in what's handed to them right away.

In short, most of them have the tendency to be lazy and to just slack off and think that the first thing they know is already the truth. As they say, there are times when truth comes on a first come, first served basis—but reality is far more different than that.

It's so hard when my memories of my death are tainted—because the people responsible tainted them, but I'll get all of them back soon. I'll be able to take all of them down, make them pay for their sins and be sorry for how each of them treated me. Payback's a bitch, you know?

I have no idea how Emmy will believe in me.

I have no idea how you will believe in me.

But I know that somehow, someway, you will.

Because…you do not want to end up dead like me, do you?

Chapter 11
In The Middle

"Hi," Daniel greeted Emmy as he arrived in their house that evening from work. He gave her a peck on the forehead, "How's your day, beautiful?"

She laughed despite herself. "I'm alright," she said. "Someone missed you, too." She told him, pertaining to Wendy, who was now curled on the floor, waiting for Daniel to pet her.

"And I missed you, too, darling girl!" Daniel said as he picked Wendy up from the floor and petted her, "I brought home your favorite wet food, too!" He smiled and led Emmy and Wendy towards the dining room.

They prepared Wendy's food for her then proceeded to eat the food that Daniel brought home for the two of them—fish and chips and some watermelon juice that Emmy liked a lot. "So," he said, "remember that client I was telling you about? The one who wanted a lot of fireplaces in her house? Her interior decorator told me that she now wants to put lots of fur rugs and lots of curtains at home. It's like she's asking for trouble, you know?"

"Some people really have weird fetishes," Emmy said while taking a bite of fish.

"Fetishes, huh? he teased and they both laughed. "Wait…you said there was something you were going to tell me about, right? What is it?"

"Oh, uh…" Emmy hesitated for a second, not wanting to ruin the mood, but then she decided that she had to tell Daniel about the problem because she was also extremely bothered already, "Well…Bree came by earlier."

"Bree?" he said, "You mean, the sister of the woman who died last night?"

"Yep, that Bree."

"What did she do here? Are you okay?"

"Yeah, I'm fine, Dan. She just…well, she asked for help regarding what happened to Angeline. She said that there's something the police don't know, and that maybe I could help her out, since she found out about everything that happened before, you know, with Lena and all…" She took a deep breath, "Anyway, she was adamant in saying that Tyler had something to do with it."

"That's really sketchy, though. I mean, if she was that adamant, then maybe it's her who's hiding something. Just like how Tripp wanted to know the truth about her daughter's death when he was actually behind it all along."

"I know," Emmy answered, "but there's more to it than that…" She sighed and added, "Tyler was here, too."

"What?!" Daniel was even more surprised. "Like, they came together?"

"No," Emmy said, "he came on his own. He also wants me to help him, saying he heard about what I was able to do for Sky Valley in the past… and he said that he's not convinced about what the police ruled out. And, get this," she went on, "he said that he believes Bree has something to do with Angeline's murder."

"What the hell?" Daniel said. "Wow, that's…that's weird."

"I know," she answered, "and now I'm torn."

"You could have nothing to do with this, you know? Because… well, you really have nothing to do with this to be exact."

"I know," she said, "but still…" she sighed, "there's something else."

"What do you mean? Like, Angeline came back from the dead and asked you for help?" He quipped.

"Not Angeline," she answered, "Lucy."

"Lucy?" Daniel was confused. "Who's Lucy?"

"Remember that ghost I told you about last night; the ghost that I saw? That's Lucy. She showed herself to me again earlier. Even Wendy could feel her, you know? It was because of Wendy that I found her again.

Daniel didn't know whether to believe Emmy or not, especially because he's really not keen on ghosts and the like, but he decided to listen to his wife.

"Dan, she asked me for help, too."

"And why would that be? What has she got to do with all of these?"

"She's Bree and Angeline's cousin. She also knows Tyler. She…she said that Bree killed her; that she wants justice for her and for Angeline. She said that I was the only one who could help her."

"But honey, this isn't your job."

"I know that, Dan," she said, "but…but how could I say no? I mean, Lucy doesn't even know me personally and she tried all her might to show herself to me, because she knows that I could help her. How could I fail her?"

"Em,"

"No, wait," she realized that she had to look for the dress that Bree spilt something on.

"Emmy, where are you going?" Dan asked and stood to follow his wife.

She then went to the laundry room and rummaged through the hamper to look for the dress. Thankfully, she found the dress right away. She noticed that some of the stains were still on the dress and she held it up for her husband to see. "Lucy told me that those marks are poison."

"Honey, listen," he said as he took the dress from Emmy and held her by the shoulders, "You don't know about that."

"But I couldn't just sit here and not do anything. What if Lucy's right, you know?" She asked. "I need to figure this out."

"But why?"

"For the same reason that we figured out what really happened to Annabeth before: For justice. For…I don't know. Don't you want me to do this?"

Daniel took a deep breath. "I have faith in you, Em," he said, "but…that doesn't mean that you should get yourself caught up in this mess. None of this is your fault."

"I know that," she said, "but that also doesn't mean that I should just choose to have nothing to do with it. They're asking me for help. It means they know I could make things better for them."

He took a deep breath and closed his eyes, then kissed his wife softly on the lips. "Okay," he said, "Okay," He went on, "but for now, you should rest. I heard that Adam Brody flick you still haven't seen is on so—"

"Yeah, I'll be with you in a second."

Daniel then made his way to the den and Emmy knew right at that moment that things will certainly be changing.

She only hoped for the best.

I know the feeling of people not believing you. It's not the nicest thing in the world, you know?

Once upon a time, I was the kind of girl who wished for the world and believed in everything. I was the kind of girl who believed that she could get what she wanted if she put her whole heart into it.

But you know what?

I didn't only get my heart broken, I lost everything, too.

Everything.

Hmm. That is a big word. I lost my life, alright, but what else did I really lose?

Nothing.

My parents never treated me fairly, mainly because I wasn't a boy and because I wasn't pretty enough—I'm just your average ordinary girl. The boy I loved, the boy who mattered much to me…I thought I mattered a lot to him, too, but he never even visited my grave or whatever. My friends? Oh, please, like they actually cared about me?!

I wouldn't be here if it weren't for them.

So, I guess, dying isn't really the saddest thing in life.

The saddest thing in life is dying knowing that nobody really cared about you the way you want them to.

The saddest thing in life is knowing that you didn't matter; that your death didn't even have much effect on the people you cared for.

That could make you feel more broken than anything else in the world.

Chapter 12
You Know What To Do

"Emmy, Emmy, wake up..."

Emmy stirred in her sleep and opened her eyes to a blinding light. She was no longer in her bed. The surroundings were full of roses and thorns, of flowers of every kind.

She had been here before.

She wouldn't forget.

It was the same place where Ruby and Annabeth talked to her in her dreams before. It was a land filled with mystery—but also of hope.

"Ruby?" she asked, stepping on the cold, cobblestoned floor, "Ruby, Annabeth? Are you here?"

"You're still very smart, Emmy," Ruby said behind her.

Emmy turned around and saw Ruby. She thought that Ruby looked different now—like she wasn't the same person she dreamed about before. Her curly red hair was beautiful and polished, her lips were ruby red and she wore the cleanest, purest and whitest dress possible. She looked like she was finally at peace.

"Ruby, it's you."

Ruby laughed, "You bet it's me." She grinned. "I don't fancy seeing you here, Em. I thought you finally found peace."

Emmy took a deep breath. "I thought so, too," She muttered.

Ruby led her to the bench near the well. They sat down and Ruby spoke. "You can let go right away, you know?" she said. "But of course, you'd choose to help them all out because well, that's you. That's not really a bad thing, except that it's intruding on your life already."

"I couldn't just let all of them down."

Ruby sighed, "Of course." She rolled her eyes.

"Do you know anything about this, Ruby?" Emmy asked. "I mean…have you ever spoken to Lucy before—"

"Yeah, I know her." Ruby said, "Crazy girl, that one, but I couldn't say I don't understand her, you know?" She sighed. "Anyway, you already know what to do, Em."

"What?"

"You know it. You just have to figure it out. And be careful because everything isn't everything. You know that."

A flash of blinding light again and Emmy woke up, feeling all the more confused.

Ghosts are more powerful than you think they are.

Not all of them, of course, but you know what? When they work together, just like people do, they can do a lot of things.

Seriously though, I have no idea what Emmy's being confused about. It's like, everything she has to know is already handed to her, you know?

But oh well, sometimes, the more things are just handed to you like that, the more confusing they could be.

I just wish she'd figure things out sooner.

Oh, wait, she's now walking her husband out the door. Guess I have to talk to her again now.

Chapter 13
She's Dangerous

"Are you sure you're going to be okay?" Daniel asked Emmy as they were by the front door. "I could take the day off."

"I'll be fine, Dan. I'll probably just look for something I could check the dress with.

"I see." Daniel answered. "Call me if you need anything, okay?"

"Yeah," she answered. "Oh, uh, I had a dream about Ruby last night, by the way. I think that's a sign that...that you know, I really should move on with my life."

Daniel looked at her and took a deep breath. "Honey, I think all of these things will just stress you out. Please just..."

"Dan," She squeezed his hand, "I couldn't just go and take rest or whatever it is that you want me to do. I need to do this."

"Then you be careful." He said. "I don't want you to just...I don't know. Things are going so well between us and I really don't want you to get hurt or anything."

"I'll be okay." She said. "I promise."

He took a deep breath. "I'll call you, okay?" He said and kissed her on the lips. "I love you."

"I love you, too."

Then she bid goodbye to her husband and watched him drive away. She closed the front door and was surprised to see Lucy floating behind her. "Hi," Lucy said.

Emmy's heart beat faster and then she rolled her eyes. "Why don't you show yourself when my husband is around?" She then made her way to the cleaning supplies cabinet and got some old pieces of cloth to wipe the tables with.

"I told you," Lucy said, "It's not that easy. And I don't really need his help, I need yours."

Emmy rolled her eyes. "I had a dream involving Ruby last night, you know? She said she knows you."

"Of course she does." She said sarcastically. "It's a big party up there for us ghosts. I'd ask you to join but then again…"

"Can you stop being so creepy?"

"Sorry." Lucy said. "What did she tell you?"

"That I already know what to do." Emmy sighed as she wiped the windows. She then looked at Lucy. "Seriously, you ghosts are so cryptic!"

"Because that's the truth, Em," Lucy said, "You already know what to do. You got to hand that dress in, but before that, you have to figure out why all these happened."

"If that's what should be done then why don't you do it yourself?"

"Duh," Lucy expressed. "You already know the answer to that. Come on."

"This is just so crazy, you know! Like, who would believe me when I say that a ghost is the reason why I'm doing all these things? And besides, how do you even know that Bree really did this?"

"It's because Bree is dangerous."

"Yeah? How so?"

Lucy sighed. "I'm trying so hard not to scream, you know?"

"Stop being such a kid."

"Well, I am a kid, at least, in human terms. I was only 17 when I died, 2 weeks short of my 18th birthday, a couple of days before my high school graduation." She then went on to face Emmy even better. "Bree's always been a bitch."

"Just because someone's a bitch doesn't mean she's already evil."

"But she is." Lucy said. "How else can you explain her tormenting me when we were teenagers because I didn't have the nicest clothes, even if we actually let her live in our house? How else can you explain her taking Tyler away from me?"

"Taking Tyler away from you? What do you mean?" Emmy asked. "Were you and Tyler together before?"

"That's complicated."

Emmy laughed. "Really now? You're using that word on me? Like, none of this is complicated?"

"Think what you want to think but you know you're smarter than this, Emmy."

"Whatever."

"Why don't you ask Bree what that thing on your dress is?"
Emmy took a deep breath just as the phone rang. It was her dad, just checking in to say hello.

"Hi, daddy," Emmy greeted.

"How are you, Em? Are things good?"

"Yeah, everything's fine." Emmy hoped that she didn't sound unsure, especially because Lucy was still puttering around her.

"You don't sound like it. Do you want me to drop by?"

"No, dad, everything's okay." She said and took a deep breath. "It's just… what if people ask you for help even if you have nothing to do with something, but then you know that you could actually help them? Would you really help them, or would you opt to just stay on your own, go back the normal route and all that?"

"Well, it always depends on the situation." Troy said, "But you know…as they say, when you know that you could help someone out, why don't you, right? But then again, if it's too dangerous…you know, you could always try to keep it safe. What is this about, anyway?"

"Nothing," Emmy said abruptly, "Nothing, really. I'll just…I'll see you soon, okay? Give my regards to Audrina."

"I will." Troy said. "Love you, kiddo."

"I love you, too, Dad."

The phone call ended then Emmy dialed Bree's number.

"Would you come here as soon as you can? I'd like to talk to you."

There are some people who get things so easily. They don't know the slightest thing about hardship and perseverance.

I guess you could say that for Bree.

When she came into our lives, she owned everything, like we're the ones who owe her. She thought of everything and everyone as her own.

I don't know if that's some kind of a defense mechanism or what, but that's how she was.

And you know what?

People loved her. People looked up to her, bowed to her, and treated her like a queen when she didn't deserve to be treated that way.

She went to school one day and voila! She became the most popular person our age. She had people begging to be her friends. She had boys lining up to be with her. She had power and she knew it.

But I guess that's how life goes some days.

Life is in under no contract to be fair to you. You take what's handed to you, and you try to manage. You try to live life like you're supposed to, not the way you want to.

Sometimes though, you wish that the world would change, things would go off track, and you can be the person you always wanted to be, without anyone ever noticing the metamorphosis, so that they won't feel like you can't change, so they'll see you as a brand new person.

Maybe, that was how it was for Bree.

Maybe, in California, she wasn't the rich, popular girl. After all, they had to move back to Sky Valley because the cost of living in California was taking its toll on her mom.

Maybe, she wasn't the girl everybody wanted so she worked her way to the top, even though it doesn't seem that way because she was mean, and cunning, and well...brave enough to do the things she did.

In a way, I wish I could still do that and that could still happen for me.

But I guess, it no longer will.

I'm trying to understand Bree, but whenever I remember what happened to me, I just couldn't.

I guess, I never really will.

Chapter 14
Uncovering The Tracks

"I'm just asking you what was in your hip flask that night. You know, when you spilled some of its contents on me and you were suddenly in panic mode." "I wasn't panicking." Bree said stiffly as she drank some chamomile tea that Emmy made. "I was just…I was sorry."

"I get that, Bree. But it sure looked as if you were scared of something."

Bree took a deep breath. "What are you doing, Emmy? Why are you asking me this? What does this have to do with Angeline's death?"

"I don't know." Emmy said. "I'm just asking."

"Where's the dress, anyway?"

"It's in the laundry." Emmy said. "Why? Shouldn't I wash it?"

"No, of course not," Bree said. "That's ridiculous." She went on. "It's just… pumpkin juice, that's what's in the hip flask, okay? I spiked it with booze because…because I knew that Tyler was going to propose to Angeline that night. And…you know, whatever happens, I just thought it would be good to celebrate with her. Or, drink with her because she's nervous and all. My sister could be frantic at times."

"But I saw your face when they got engaged." Emmy said, "You didn't look like you were happy."

"Of course," Bree answered, "I mean…my sister's getting married. Of course, I have the right to be emotional right?"

"That's it? That's just it? And not because you have feelings for Tyler?"

"Don't be so absurd." Bree said, her grip on the tea cup so stiff, Emmy thought the cup was going to break any second then. "Oh this is all Lucy's fault!"

"What did you just say?" Emmy asked, confused.

"Nothing." Bree said and took a deep breath. "You know what? I'm going home. I'll just…I'll see you around."

Bree stood up and bumped into one of the walls then made her way out the door, determined not to look back.

***

Later that day, it was Tyler's turn to talk to Emmy.

"So…" Emmy asked him, after drinking some juice, "Did anyone know about your plans of asking Angeline marry you that evening?"

"The restaurant manager, of course," He said. "and those musicians. It's funny how your husband asked them to sing, too. There must have been a lot of money for them that night." He laughed nervously. "Anyway…besides them, and Angeline's parents, there was no one else who knew."

"Not even her sister? Bree?"

"No." Tyler said. "I figured that if Bree knew, she'd…she'd do something."

"You mean, kill Angeline?"

"Yeah," he said. "She is…she could have quite a temper. I told you, she is a nice person but she has her quirks just like the rest of us."

"So…if she didn't know about your plans then why would you invite her to eat out with you guys?"

"Truth be told, she really wasn't invited per se." He said. "It's just that…it was her birthday the following day and…and she said she wanted to celebrate with us. She told Angeline that and of course, since Angeline didn't know about my plans, she agreed. Angeline's nice that way, although sometimes, she also hates that Bree's always third-wheeling and all that. But I think she also felt sad for Bree because she's also lost a lot in life and…and no one really thought that she would be the one who'd end up without a partner."

"It's because you had a past, right?"

66

Tyler sighed. "It's complicated." He said. "Nothing's ever black and white in this town."

"Oh yeah, I've heard that one before."

"I'm serious." He said. "It's…things haven't really been great for us since…since Lucy died."

"Lucy?" Emmy asked, pretending that she doesn't know Lucy.

"Bree's cousin. She died when…when we were almost out of high school. No one really knows what happened. The police said it was accidental drowning, in the toilet, you know…because she was wasted and all. But…I don't think it was just that. Someone pushed her down, I feel like that's what happened."

"And that person is Bree?"

"I really don't know what to think." Tyler said. "But it wouldn't be a surprise. And for that, I'm sorry." His eyes were brimming with tears now. "I just…I just want things to be okay. I want answers. I want this all to be done. I'm sorry."

Emmy took a deep breath. "Don't worry." She said. "I think we're going to get through this. But I have to talk to someone first."

Remember when I told you that the truth isn't always what it seems?

Yeah, well, I guess I've been trolling around, too. Forgive me.

So, you see…It's really Bree who killed Angeline. But…it wasn't her fault alone. I did it, too.

How could I when I'm dead and all that?

Well…let's just say that being dead doesn't necessarily mean that you could no longer be around. It only means that you're not physically seen by everyone, but that you could impose yourself on them when you want to.

Just like what I'm doing with Emmy.

Just like what I did with Bree.

No, she didn't see me. She chose not to. But I played with her mind, you know, and made her whacko. Made her think she was going insane.

I told her that Tyler never liked her.

I told her that Tyler won't have feelings for her, ever.

I told her that soon, Tyler and Angeline were going to get engaged and it would be the end of whatever fantasies she had with Tyler. That it would be the end of things, so she should try to stop it if she actually wants to get together with Tyler.

After all, I'm already dead, you know? I couldn't do anything with Tyler anymore, but she still could.

I wasn't rooting for her, though.

I just wanted her to end Angeline's life because I wanted her to be in jail. I want her to rot in jail and go to hell.

At least then, I'd get some of the peace that I deserve.

Or at least, that's what I thought.

Real life's always more complicated than that, even for us ghosts.

Chapter 15
Tell Me The Truth

"Lucy? Where are you?" Emmy looked for Lucy again after she got to talk to Bree and Tyler that afternoon. She wanted to know the truth and she knew that Lucy could tell her. She knew that there were still a lot of things Lucy wasn't telling her about.

She opened the door to their bedroom. There she found Lucy looking out the window, crying.

"There you are." Emmy said. "What are you doing here? Why are you crying?"

"Don't I have the right to cry?"

"I didn't say that." Emmy said. "You're so full of secrets, you know?"

Lucy looked at her and bit her lip. "You already know what you know."

"But it's still not enough." Emmy answered. "I always thought you were hiding something from me. You're kind of a weird ghost, Lucy, barging into my life like that and not telling me everything I really need to know, and you expect me to help you? What are you hiding?"

Lucy was crying harder now. Emmy didn't think that it was possible for ghosts to cry like that, or to have those big emotions for any reason.

"Look," Emmy said, "I don't want you to cry like that and be sad, Lucy. I actually want to help you. But you need to tell me everything I need to know."

"Bree killed her, okay? She killed Angeline. She spiked that pumpkin juice not only with booze, but also with poison. End of story."

"That's obvious." Emmy told her. "But there's something more. I mean, it's just so obvious, Emmy. You're lying to me about something."

69

"And what would that something be?"

"That you actually have something to do with this?"

"How could I when I'm dead?"

"Well, you were able to show yourself to me, and you don't even know me. So, how could you not show yourself to Bree whom you've known all your life? You were cousins. And, she said it's your fault."

"Because she's insane!" Lucy shouted.

"Really? That's it?"

"Fine!" Lucy said, the air in the room getting colder. "Fine, okay? She couldn't see me because she doesn't want to! But she felt me. She heard me. And… and I thought, maybe, I could play with her mind. Twist her mind in such a way that she'd feel sorry for the things she did in the past. I wanted her to feel crazy, be insane. I wanted to ruin her. So, I told her that Tyler has plans of marrying Angeline and of course, that wrecked her. She's been in love with him for so long, you know? She's loved him ever since she came here from California. She knew that I liked him but she was like…she acted like she owned him. She was a bitch through and through."

"Then I died. I died and all their worlds became crazy and they've been whacked by guilt and sadness. She thought that Tyler would find solace in her, but alas! He thought that Angeline was better, she was nice and innocent and could do no wrong, and that she was someone better to talk to, unlike Bree."

"I reminded her of all those things. I reminded her of the things that hurt because no matter how good a person is, when she's hurt, she could do the worst things imaginable. So, I played with her brain until she couldn't take it anymore. I told her the best kind of poison to use and told her that she should go kill Angeline."

"And the crazy girl did just that."

For a while, Emmy couldn't speak. She was shocked. She didn't know how to feel about it.

"I know you think I'm evil." Lucy said. "I guess I am. But…but I just didn't

70

know how to avenge myself and I thought…I thought that ruining their lives would…would make things better because somehow, I could prove that Bree's capable of this."

"Oh god," Emmy said, feeling her head was going to explode, "oh my god, Lucy. What have you done?"

"Em…"

Emmy shook her head. "I guess we'll just do what needs to be done then." She then picked up the phone and called some of her friends from the police station. "Yes, yes, I could bring it right now." She nodded her head, "I'll be there in a few. Could you call Tyler Montgomery, too? I need to talk to him. No, no, don't arrest him. Yes, see you."

"You better be thankful that you're a ghost." Emmy told Lucy as went out of the room, and closed the door behind the confused ghost inside.

When I saw Bree poisoning that drink, I knew she was in it for the haul.

If there's something about Bree, it's that she never gives up, especially when her happiness, no matter how unselfish it seemed, was at stake. And I guess, in that way, we shared something.

If you're going to ask me if I'm happy right now, I have to tell you that even if what I wanted came to life, it's still not enough.

Somehow, I feel like I owe Angeline a great deal. She was the nicest of all of the… you know? She didn't deserve what she got.

But as I've told you earlier, that's life. You never really get what you think you deserve. Sometimes, all you get are scraps out of the lives of people who mean nothing. All you get is stupidity and sadness and things you don't really want, but are the consequences of your actions.

In death, just like in life, you have to be careful with what you wish for. Because sometimes, even if you think you'd already get what you want, you know that it's never really like that.

And for that, I'm sorry.

Chapter 16
Entrapment

Bree didn't know what Tyler was doing in her house. She knew that some-how, he knew what she did to Angeline. But what was he doing there?

It wasn't my fault anyway, she thought, Lucy made me do this. Lucy made me do this because she believes that I killed her. But…in a way, she did me a favor. At least now, Angeline's not around anymore. And I could finally have Tyler.

But what is he doing here?

"I made that for you." Bree told Tyler as she handed him a cup of lemon tea. "Sorry…I…do you want anything else?"

It was the day of Angeline's funeral and everyone else was at church.

"No, I just wanted to pass time before, you know…" Tyler said. "It's still kind of surreal knowing she'll be buried today. I couldn't believe it."

"I'm really sorry." Bree said, squeezing Tyler's cold hand. "I wish it didn't happen."

"Yeah." Tyler said. "But maybe, it's for the best."

This came as a surprise to Bree. Why would Tyler say that, she thought?

"What do you mean?" Bree asked.

Tyler drank some tea then answered. "I'm just saying…it's as if things have been a little crazy from the get go." He said. "I mean, I did love her, you know? She was amazing, you know she was, but…but I guess I also pressured myself into marrying her. I mean, do you actually think that I'm ready, Bree?"

"I don't know," Bree said. This felt like a miracle. Maybe, she should thank Lucy now because at least, she could now have Tyler for herself and it now feels like Tyler's beginning to realize that, too. "But maybe…maybe you're right. I mean, it's never too late to start over."

"Tell me something," Tyler said, "You had something to do with Angeline's death, right?"

"Tyler…I…" Bree didn't know what to say. She knew she was on the losing end of this, but then again, how could she not trust Tyler? And, this was her one and only chance to come clean. "Yes." She muttered. "But I didn't do it just because I hate her. She's my sister. I did it because…because it was the right thing to do."

"Right," Tyler said and at that moment, he looked her in the eyes and inched his face closer to hers. He then slowly kissed her on the lips, the moment fluttering in her mind like something she couldn't believe in, but she allowed herself to be submerged in his kisses, because that's what she had wanted all along. And now that Angeline's gone, her dreams could finally come true.

Just then, the door opened and in came Emmy together with her husband, Daniel, and some people she didn't know, but she recognized were from the police station. What the hell's going on?

"Emmy? What are you doing here? Tyler!"

Tyler spat on the floor. "I'm disgusted in you, Bree." Tyler said. "If the police weren't here, you'd probably be dead by now."

"What?"

One of the policemen then gave Emmy the dress that she was wearing the night of Tyler and Angeline's engagement, the one that Bree stained.

"Oh, my god I thought you had that cleaned already?!"

"Nope," Emmy said, "Because I'm smarter than you think I am, Bree." She went on, "I had the authorities check this, and they found some traces of poison on this dress, Bree."

"So? That's not my fault."

"Really?" Emmy said. "What if I tell you that your whole conversation with

74

Tyler just seconds ago has just been recorded? You just admitted that you killed Angeline, Bree. When will you stop lying?"

At that moment, Bree felt like her world has just come to an end. She felt like everything she worked hard for was now out of the window and things could never be okay again. She tried to remember how it all got to this and how her world became this dark and this crazy.

"Miss Bree Lawson, you are under arrest for the murder of Miss Angeline Lawson. You have the right to an attorney…"

She tried to make them understand, and all she could say was she was sorry.

I kind of feel sorry for Bree, you know?

Well, not just for her, but for every person in this world, and in any world, whoever loved and wasn't loved back, at least not the way they wanted to be loved back.

Love is the best and worst thing there is. Love is the most powerful thing of all, because it doesn't only bring happiness with it, it also brings forth sadness and confusion as well as hatred and anger. It brings with it a lot of things that you could no longer tell what is wrong and what is right.

Of course, you know the differences between right and wrong, but there are moments in life when you couldn't help yourself do the things you're not supposed to do because you're overcome with emotion.

I guess that's what happened to Bree.

I guess that's what happened to me.

When you let anger control you, when you forget the things that have already happened in the past, when you think that you're way beyond everything, you ruin your chances of living or dying normally.

You ruin everything.

And that's never a good thing.

No, it's never good at all.

Chapter 17
Poison Ivy

Bree was alone in the office one evening. She was about to go home, fixing her things on the table, when the lights suddenly flickered, and she was taken aback because this kind of thing never happened before.

Maybe, it did. It did happen, just a couple of days after Lucy died years ago, but then again, that was a lifetime ago and she didn't know why this would happen again. She wanted to get out of the room fast but then she heard Lucy's voice. As weird and hollow as it sounds, she knew it was Lucy. She'd still recognize her voice anywhere, no matter how much time has passed.

"Scared aren't you?" Lucy asked.

"I'm not scared of you, Lucy. Go away."

"Yeah, but you're shaking, pretty little Bree. You're so scared and so in fear. Why? Because you know I could hurt you now?" Lucy laughed. It was a maniacal, evil laugh, shrilling through the walls that Bree wished someone would hear.

"You can't hurt me, you're dead!"

"But of course. You killed me."

"Lucy, I swear to God, I didn't kill you. I've done a lot of things in my life but I never killed you. What happened is way beyond me."

"But you were happy, right? You didn't even grieve for me! You never cried for me, Bree, when all I've done is been good to you and your mother!"

"Leave my mother out of this!"

"Yeah? Who cares? You're both stupid. You both didn't appreciate the help we gave you!"

"What do you want?!" Bree called out.

"Justice." Lucy said.

Just then, someone opened the door and asked Bree if she was okay. She hastily ran out of the room, never wanting to come back.

***

"Lovely dress, Bree, really lovely."

Bree was shocked to hear Lucy's voice again. She was dressing up for a party that evening but now wanted to just stay in bed, or go as far away from Lucy as she could.

"What the hell do you want?" Bree said through gritted teeth.

"It's actually you who needs something from me."

"What would I need from you?"

"Well, just so you know, I saw Tyler buying a ring earlier. He even talked to one of his friends and said that he was going to ask Angeline to marry him on Saturday next week. You know, the day before your birthday. I just thought you should know."

Bree stopped in her tracks. She couldn't deny the fact that she still had feelings for Tyler, strong feelings actually. *"What do you mean?"*

"They're getting engaged, damn it."

"No."

"Yes they are." Lucy said. *"And you know what? It's over for you!"*

"Of course it's not! He doesn't love her!"

"Then keep her out of the equation."

"What does that mean?"

"Oh don't play dumb with me, Bree. It means you should do to Angeline what you did to me. You should kill her."

"But I didn't kill you, Lucy. How many times do I have to tell you that?"

"I don't care." Lucy said. "Kill Angeline, Bree. Kill her and you'll get everything that you want."

"You hate me, Lucy, why should I listen to you?"

"Because…sometimes, it's good for a ghost to have fun. And besides, I also couldn't forgive Angeline for being with him. She has no respect for me, for my memory."

"So, you're jealous?"

"Like you are."

Bree scoffed. "I have to go."

"Oh, believe me, Bree, you'll thank me soon."

***

"Still haven't gotten around to making that poison, huh?"

It's 5 days before Bree's birthday, and 4 days before the engagement. Lucy was coaxing her, letting her fall into her trap.

"You know…you can always spike pumpkin juice with booze. Add some cyanide and poison ivy, or your choice of poison and it could become deadly. Throw the hip flask away, and you're free, Bree. You can have Tyler for yourself. Thank me after."

***

"Hey, Anj," Bree said while she and Angeline were watching TV one afternoon, three days before the engagement. "You have any plans for Saturday?"

"Saturday? Yeah, Tyler asked me out on a date, I mean, it's been a while since we last had enough time for each other. You know how busy he could

get sometimes. "

"Aw, that sucks." Bree said. "I thought we could you know, spend some time together coz it's my birthday on Sunday, you know, and...well..."

Angeline felt like she would be wrong if she told her sister no. After all, they're the only ones who were there for each other now. Their mother was in Cambodia, their friends were almost non-existent and she couldn't let her sister down.

"You know what?" Angeline said, "Why don't you just come with us? It'll be fun. I'm sure Ty won't mind." She smiled, looking as pure and angelic as could be.

"Are you sure?"

"Of course." Angeline smiled. "Of course."

***

Bree took a deep breath as she laced the drink with poison. She was in one of the cubicles in the powder room the evening of the engagement. Her heart was pounding; she was in pain.

She knew she should be excited, but she wasn't.

She didn't know how to feel.

This was her sister she's going to kill.

But then again, her chances of being happy will be higher if Angeline's no longer around. She closed the hip flask which was brimming with fluid now and got out of the cubicle where she bumped into Emmy. She knows her for being the person who kicked Lena McMahon out of Sky Valley.

She bumped into her and spilled a little something on her dress, and Emmy wasn't sure what it was. She only saw that it came inside the woman's intricately designed small hip flask, smaller than the usual ones you see in the market.

"Oh, gosh!" Bree said. "Oh my goodness, I'm sorry."

"It's okay." Emmy said. "I'm fine. It's nothing."

"No...it's..." Bree sighed. "I'm really sorry, I wasn't looking."

"It's okay." Emmy said and smiled. "Look, it doesn't even show." She laughed.

Bree smiled back nervously. "Uh, I should go." She said. "Sorry again."

***

Bree's heart hurt as she saw Angeline's sparkling diamond ring, and how Angeline's face lit up when she talked about the ring and about being engaged.

"Can you believe this, Bree?" Angeline said. "I'm getting married!"

"Of course you are."

"But...but aren't you happy for me?"

Bree laughed. "How can I not be happy for you? You're my sister." She then took the hip flask from her purse. "And this calls for a celebration."

"Oh no, I..."

"Come on, Anj, just one drink."

Angeline laughed, "Okay then." She said, took the hip flask from her sister, and drank. She drank and drank until she could no longer breathe, her mind getting cloudy, her joints stiff.

"Bree... what..."

But before she could finish her sentence, she fell down to the floor, leaving Bree dumbstruck for a second.

She then realized that she couldn't let people see her that way. She took the hip flask, flushed the contents in the toilet, and threw the flask in, knowing it would be submerged anyway, because she had it custom-made for the occasion.

"Sorry." She muttered, no longer feeling like herself.

Then, she decided to position herself on the floor and hold her sister, like the grieving sister she should be.

"AHHHHHHHHH!!!!" She screamed, mustering all the painful emotions that she could, so she could get people's attention and let them see her as a victim, too.

She didn't kill her sister, that's what she would tell them.

She didn't kill her sister.

For what it's worth, I led Bree to this.

You already know how I wanted to seek revenge and how I wanted justice. But...somehow, I know that I still won't get that justice, at least not anytime soon.

Because...no matter how I make myself believe that Bree's responsible for my death, the truth is that I don't know anything at all.

Because if I really was going to be honest with you, then I guess you should know that I clearly have no idea who my killer was. I still have no idea who killed me.

And that's what I want to find out.

See?

The truth is really so much bigger than what we make it to be.

Chapter 18
It Ain't Over 'Til It's Over

After Bree was taken to the police station, and after a series of questionings, Emmy was invited by Angeline's mother to Angeline's funeral. She didn't decline, because she thought that it would be right to give them this chance to talk to her, ask her what she knows, though she wasn't entirely sure if they'd believe the Lucy bit. She really didn't know if she should tell about Lucy, actually.

Daniel opted out of it, saying he had to do something. Emmy was a bit disappointed but then again, she knew that life had to go on, even amidst the craziest stuff like this one.

Emmy thought the funeral was beautiful, no matter how sad it was. At least, Angeline would be laid to rest in peace. She threw a daisy on her grave and muttered a prayer, hoping that she'd actually forgive Lucy for what she did, and Bree for having the guts to put Lucy's thoughts to life.

Somehow, Emmy felt like her life had taken a 180 degree turn again. But maybe, this was part of her purpose in life. Maybe, even if she wanted to run away from this town and let people do their own jobs and not care about anything anymore, she knew that she wouldn't be able to do it. Because, more often than not, life has other plans, and you have to try your very best to survive.

"Thank you," Angeline's mother told her, in tears, as Angeline was laid to rest. "I'm still coming to terms with this, but…thank you."

Emmy didn't know what to say but she just let Angeline's mother give her a hug. She knew that it was the least she could do, knowing how hard it is to lose a daughter, and having another daughter locked up because she was the cause of her own sister's demise. It probably was one of the worst things in life, and Emmy really felt sorry for all of them.

"Call me if you need anything." Emmy told her. "It's the least I could do."

The sun was shining bright and Tyler asked her if he could bring her home.

She declined, opting to walk. After all, her house wasn't that far away, and she wanted to be alone.

She thought about all the times in her life when she thought she knew everything, but she turned out wrong. She thought about all the times when she thought a happy ending was already a happy ending, but she was wrong. But then again, maybe that's part of life's surprises, and twists, and everything else that makes it what it is. And if she was going to ask herself, she wouldn't have it any other way.

When she arrived home, she was surprised to find Wendy jumping on her, wanting to be petted. Wendy led her to the dining room where Daniel was waiting for her, a bouquet of sunflowers in his hand, and a feast waiting for her on the table.

"Daniel, what—"

"I thought I'd make a detour before going back to work." He smiled. "I'm so proud of you." He said, handing her the flowers.

"Dan," she smiled, "Thank you."

"You always prove how amazing and generous and loving you are. This is the least I could do."

"You didn't have to."

"But I wanted to." He said. "I love you."

"I love you, too."

They kissed and ate and enjoyed the moment. Later, Daniel had to go back to work for a bit, so Emmy led him to the front door and watched him drive away. She closed the door and was about to go to the kitchen when she saw Lucy, looking every bit as sad as could be.

"Lucy?" She said. "What... what are you still doing here?"

"You've got to help me, Emmy."

"What do you mean?"

"Emmy…I…I wasn't completely honest with you." She cried. "I don't know who my real killer is. Please, help me."

"What?"

Dangerous Teas & Treats

Chapter 19
The Tea Party

(7 years ago)

It was a beautiful, sun-shiny day at the Sky Valley Clubhouse. Women were dressed in colorful frocks and pearls, men donned suits as if they're from some other era.

"Looking good, Angeline." Don Darmer told Angeline, who was then eating a piece of mango macaroon. Don was her friend, Libby's boyfriend at that time. He was a suave guy who knew that his good looks meant a lot—and could drive him to great success.

"Thanks, Don." Angeline said. "Where's Libby?"

"Oh, she's just—"

"I'm here." Libby said giddily. She seemed drunk, like someone just spiked her tea. "This tea is gooooooooood." She hiccupped.

"Are you drunk?" Angeline asked. Her brunette locks held up by flowers in her hair. "Libs, this isn't the place for that."

"Of course this isn't the place for that." Bree said sarcastically. "You're such a prude, Angeline."

"And apparently, you're drunk, too." Angeline rolled her eyes. "Can't you at least respect this event? Our mom is part of the committee."

"Oh believe me, Anj, she'd also be drinking once she gets home. Why not start for her now?"

"You are so funny, Harper," Lucy then said as she was walking towards the group. She was trying not to trip in her heavy yellow dress that was full of ribbons and feathers. She was walking with Harper and Laurel, two of their friends who have been together since the last prom. This surprised them all as Laurel has always been quiet and focused on her studies, while Harper has always been the easy-go-lucky guy, just like the rest of his friends. "Isn't he super funny?" Lucy continued.

"Look who's so wasted!" Bree laughed. "I didn't know you had it in you, Luce."

"Are you kidding me, Bree?" Lucy said. "You spiked my tea!"

"You allowed me to!"

"Where's Tyler, by the way?" Bree asked. She was now worried because it's been a couple of minutes since she last saw Tyler.

"I have no idea." Lucy answered. "He's probably kissing one of his girls." She hiccupped.

"Shut Up." Bree seethed.

Just then, Tyler went up to the group, a weird smile on his face. "Hi, guys." He said as he tousled his hair. "Bree, can we talk?"

"Now?" Bree said. "Honey, I'm spiked. Can we do it later, then?"

"But—"

"She's right," Laurel said. "You can't possibly talk to Bree when she's not in the right state of mind."

"Why are you being so harsh?" Bree asked.

"I was only trying to help." Laurel answered. "Anyway, it's getting late. Are we still on for the sleepover?"

"Obviously." Libby answered. "Let Don drive us home. The rest of you guys can go. Sorry, losers." She winked and they made the long walk towards Don's van that will then take them to Libby's house in Cherry Street.

***

"You know, sometimes I wonder why Lucy here never gets a boyfriend." Bree said as she was sitting down on one of the couches in Libby's house. It was one of the biggest houses in town, so they almost always hold their sleepovers there. Libby's feet were propped on the table in front of her, and she was drinking some chardonnay. "I think no one wants her." She mocked. "Poor little sweet Lucy, always such a loser."

"What is wrong with you, Bree?" Lucy asked, drinking some more of the spiked tea from earlier. "Why do you always have to hate on me like that? I never did anything wrong to you. And in case you've forgotten, my parents gave you a home."

"You don't have to remind me." Bree said. "You're still a loser."

"A flirt and a loser." Libby said. "I mean, she was obviously flirting with Harper earlier. Right, Laurel?"

"All you girls are drunk." Laurel replied and drank some water. "Harper loves me, I'm not jealous."

"Touché." Bree raised an eyebrow and drank some more chardonnay. "And what about little Miss Angeline here? Don was flirting with you earlier, Anj! What's up with that?"

"He was not flirting with me." Angeline said. "You're obviously drunk, Bree."

"Right," Libby said. "And besides, why would Don flirt with Angeline? She's way out of my league."

"Of course I am," Angeline said. "I'm not like the rest of you."

This made them all surprised because Angeline barely talked that way. She was always nice and quiet and patient—what in the world happened?

"What did you say?" Bree asked.

"You are a bitch, Bree." Angeline said. "I won't be surprised if Tyler's going to leave you for someone else."

"What did you just say?!"

"Hey—"Libby tried to stop them. "Hey—"

But just then, Tyler called and broke up with Bree on the phone. She couldn't believe what she just heard. She couldn't believe that Tyler would break up with her like that.

So, she found herself in tears, not really wanting to talk to anyone. But she knew she wouldn't be able to keep it for long.

"What happened?" Lucy asked.

Bree looked at all of them. "It's over." She said. "He broke up with me." And she allowed herself to be consumed by her tears.

***

The following morning was a morning they'd never forget. When they woke up from their almost endless slumber (caused by the amount of alcohol they've taken),

They would remember it as an extremely cold morning; a morning that would soon be full of mourning—and that they'd want to erase from their memories, but would haunt them for the rest of their lives.

It was Bree's shrill screams that woke everyone up. She only wanted to go to the bathroom, for her morning routine, when suddenly, she stopped in her tracks because Lucy had her head down in the toilet, puke on the faucet and on the tiled floor. Bree couldn't believe her eyes and she didn't know what to do.

"Luce?" She said to try to get Lucy's attention. Lucy wasn't moving so Bree decided that it would be better if she tapped her on the shoulder. "Lucy, what are you doing?"

Bree was in shock. Lucy was so cold; so cold that it wasn't normal.

"Lucy—" She tried to make Lucy face her but then she just fell to the floor, her body cold and hard, making the fall end with a loud thud.

"Lucy—" She cried, despite herself. "Lucy...Oh my god! Oh god!" She screamed. "Help! Help!!!!" She called out with all her might. "WHERE ARE ALL OF YOU?!!! HELP!"

There was so much pain.

Pain.

That's the very first thing that comes to mind when I think about death.

I always thought that I'd die due to old age. Or, maybe because I've been afflicted with a degenerative disease. There were times when I also thought that I'd die due to an accident; that people would mourn for me; people would consider my death as a tragedy.

Of course, it's considered a tragedy. But no one cared enough to find out what really happened because they were all contented with what the police told them. Even my parents refused to deal with the investigations anymore after the said "verdict".

They no longer live in Sky Valley. I actually have no idea where they are now but the last time I checked, they were traveling the world.

Somehow, it made me feel like they wanted me to be part of the journey, too. Because once upon a time, when I was a wee little girl, I told them that I wanted to see the world.

I know you think I'm crazy, but I find it comforting to think that my parents left Sky Valley so that in some way, they could fulfill my dreams—and be with me.

Forgive me; sometimes, I live in my fantasies.

Chapter 20
You Need To Talk To Them

(Present Day)

"Wait…" Emmy told Lucy who was then looking at her with a lot of pleading in her eyes. "Wait, so, you're telling me that it was Bree who found you at the bathroom but you're not sure that it was actually her who killed you?"

"Yes." Lucy answered meekly.

"Oh my goodness." Emmy said as she went to the kitchen and poured some food on Wendy's bowl. She then faced Lucy who seemed to be on the verge of tears. She was now getting used to Lucy being so emotional—even as a ghost. "So, you're telling me that these ideas you planted to my head all along were just lies?"

"Of course not!" Lucy explained. "Look…you have to give me some credit, okay? I…I really thought it was Bree. I mean, she had it in her. She's the kind of person who hates it when she knows that her boyfriend has an eye on others—"

"Of course she'd hate that." Emmy said as she got herself a glass of juice. "That's normal."

"Yeah, but…" Lucy sighed. "I told you, Tyler and I have a complicated history."

"Oh yeah?" Emmy asked. "That's also what he keeps on telling me, you know? So, why don't you do me a favor and tell me what the hell that actually means, will you?"

Emmy then decided that she'll make some peach pie, just so she could get her mind off things. Baking is one of those things that she was passionate about. She prepared the dough and made sure it was flaky as that would work best with peaches. Then, she combined peaches, butter, sugar, and salt altogether in a bowl and mixed them well before pouring the mixture onto the dough and covering it with another piece of dough.

After which, she went on to bake her peach pie.

She then turned to Lucy who was playing with Wendy. "A little too quiet now, aren't you?"

Lucy then diverted her attention back to Emmy. "I don't know what you want me to say."

"The truth, perhaps?"

"Fine." Lucy answered. "You want the truth? I'll give you the truth. It was me who liked him first, okay? We had been friends even before Bree and Angeline came here. We shared a lot of things…we went to school together; we were part of the Science Club, that's where we first met. Everything was going well. And…and on my 12th birthday we had a party at home. It was kind of a big deal for my parents, which I wasn't used to because they never really saw me as someone who…someone who could make them proud. In short, I never really felt like I was enough.

Anyway…that day, while we were eating cake and sharing stories in the backyard, Tyler leaned in to kiss me and…I kissed him back. It wasn't anything passionate or crazy or whatever but…but it was special because it was my first kiss. And it was his, too. We laughed afterwards, actually, and I thought everything was going great until surprise! Bree, Angeline, and their mother arrived, and my parents told me that they were going to live with us. Apparently, the party wasn't just meant for me but also for them. You know how that made me feel, Em?" She asked. "It was terrible. I had…I had to share everything again when I didn't have much to begin with. And…my parents told me to be nice to them to the point that I was prompted to…to let Bree bask in the spotlight and let Tyler think that he should be with her. I know it's stupid, but back then, more than anything, I wanted to get my parents' attention. I wanted to make them proud of me and wanted to make them see that I could make sacrifices so they would be happy; so Bree would also be happy. But then… those sacrifices weren't enough and I still lost everything.

I know you must hate me now, especially after I made you believe that I was sure it's Bree who's at fault, but I also want you to know that…that I make mistakes, too. All my life, I tried my best to be perfect but then again…I got nothing from it and now…Okay fine," She said, "I won't make any more excuses. I'm sorry. I saw Bree, I thought she was only acting when she asked for help, but I guess I'm wrong. I just…I just hope you could help me."

Emmy took a deep breath as she took the peach pie out of the oven. She then faced Lucy once more. "So," she said. "What do you want me to do then?"

"Talk to them." Lucy answered. "Talk to Bree and Tyler. Squeeze whatever you can out of them. Just please…let me know what really happened. I think I deserve to know the truth—even just that."

There are times when you think that people love you more than they show you; but then again, you realize that maybe, you couldn't always expect more: that sometimes, things are just the way they are and you have to be contented with that.

But I wasn't contented and I wanted more.

I wanted more, so that drove me to see the worst in myself and think that everyone else was better—and far more capable of being happier than me. So, I gave in to all their requests and made myself as small and invisible as can be. Little did I know that I'd permanently be invisible to the rest of them.

Chapter 21
What Have You Got To Say?

Emmy wasn't really used to going out without Daniel by her side anymore. In fact, she somehow feels that she's not complete when Daniel isn't around, but she chooses to be out on her own some days, because she knows that she can't always spend every minute with Daniel.

Today, she was meeting up with Tyler at the Orange Bistro, another one of those newly spawned restaurants in Sky Valley. Tyler was hesitant to see her, but Emmy told him that she just had a couple of questions to ask and that it wouldn't take much time.

Emmy arrived early. She almost always does, when it comes to any kind of meetings because she hates being late—and thus, she also hates people who get late. Obviously, Tyler still wasn't there.

Emmy decided to order some watermelon and chamomile tea while waiting at an outside table. She noticed that a lot has changed in Sky Valley in the past year. Like, how there were more rhododendrons than roses now; how restaurants kept popping up everywhere…and how nothing was ever really as it seemed.

Because if they were, then she probably wouldn't be helping out a ghost, right?

"Sorry," Tyler arrived, disrupting Emmy's thoughts. "I just had a couple of things to fix at home."

"It's okay." Emmy said, and motioned for the waitress to come to their table.

"Hi! Anything you want to order, sir?" She asked.

Tyler prodded over the menu and ordered a Philly Cheese Steak Sandwich and lime juice. He also asked if Emmy wanted something more but Emmy declined. Soon, their orders arrived and Emmy started to speak.

"So…" she said, "tell me a little something about your history with Bree."

Tyler drank some juice and took a deep breath. "What do you mean?"

"I mean, just tell me what I need to know."

"Why?"

"Why not?"

"Em," he said, "She's in jail now and…and I don't know how this would help."

"Well, what if I told you that this might change things?" She said. "Did you love her? When did you ever start going out?"

"It's complicated."

"Tyler," she said, "I didn't ask you to come see me just so you could say that it's complicated and all that. I just need you to tell me what I need to know."

He took a deep breath. "I didn't initially like her." He said. "Actually, Angeline and her weren't really from here but they arrived when we were around 12…It was Lucy, their dead cousin, whom I was friends with first. Lucy and I drifted apart, and Bree and I started to spend time together. By spending time together, we…we eventually became a couple. It wasn't anything serious, I mean, we were in high school."

"Serious relationships could also start in high school."

"I know," he said, "but for the most part, it was something that happened because of the situation. I mean, it seemed fitting because I was one of the popular kids, and she was one, too…so, you know…Anyway, we would break up and make up every once in a while."

"But you were together when Lucy died?"

"I…" He sighed. "I broke up with her after the tea party. I called her up and… well, I know it was a very stupid thing to do but what else could I have done?"

"And why exactly did you break up with her?"

"It's nothing."

"Really?" Emmy said. "Because you know, I think it had something to do with Lucy."

Tyler looked at her with a lot of confusion on his face. "Where did you get that idea?"

"Let's just say that I have my sources."

Tyler hesitated. "Still," he said, "it's none of your business."

"But what are you so scared about? Did you like Lucy more than you liked Bree?"

He took a deep breath. "Even if I did, what does it matter? It's been too long. Lucy's gone."

"But don't you think she deserves to know how you really feel?"

"Really, Em, what's this about? Whatever I felt about Lucy is mine and mine alone. And she's gone, okay? She's no longer coming back. Maybe, I was stupid for getting together with Bree, but I also believe that she didn't deserve the way I treated her. She also doesn't deserve being in jail. I know it's her fault but…but I feel like we're all at fault here. You don't even know how I'm feeling!" He declared and Emmy saw how he tried hard not to cry. "This is crazy enough as it is! What else do you need to know? You want to know that I'm guilty? That I feel sad? That I feel broken? Yeah, you know what? I am all of those things!" He said, "And I'm done. I don't even know why I came by." He then pulled out some cash from his pockets. "Sorry." He said as he stood up. "I have to go."

He then made his way back to his car and away from Emmy.

And somewhere, though no one was able to see her at that moment, whatever's left of Lucy's heart was breaking apart.

There are some people who are capable of breaking your heart over and over again, though they have no idea that they can.

There are some people who can tear you apart, even though they can no lon

101

ger see you.

When Tyler told me that it was me that he really liked, and that he always had feelings for me, I knew that I was the happiest at that point. But then, he broke up with Bree, and I literally had no idea what he told her...

And now, years later, he still refuses to acknowledge what he told me that day. He still refuses to talk about those things.

Why?

Because he's hurt and confused? Because he's lost a lot? Because Angeline's gone?

Sometimes, I could no longer separate truth from fiction. I could no longer understand how it all came to this.

And that thought makes me want to live my life over again and change a lot of things.

Because then, maybe, I wouldn't end up this way.

But then again, maybe not.

Chapter 22
I'm Sorry

When Emmy opened the door of the house, he was surprised to find Daniel and Wendy playing in the living room. "Hey," She said as Daniel gave her a peck on the lips. "You're here."

He laughed. "Right," he said, "I'm here." He smiled. "I bought home some of your favorite cheese fries. And an apple pie." He smiled as he led her to the kitchen, Wendy trailing behind them.

"Why are you home so early?" She said. "I just happened to be at the Orange Bistro…had a little meeting with Tyler."

"Tyler?" Daniel asked, confused. "Why? What's going on?"

"Nothing."

"Nothing?"

Emmy started to putter around the kitchen by taking pots and pans out of the cabinets and putting them back in.

Daniel then tried to get her attention again by coming up to her and letting her face him. "What's going on?" He asked.

Emmy took a deep breath as she poured herself a glass of water. "I had to talk to him, Dan." She said. "I needed to figure out the truth about his past relationships to hopefully figure out who killed Lucy."

"What?" Daniel was even more confused. "But…didn't Lucy tell you before that she knows that Bree killed her? And, that's also the reason why Bree killed Angeline, right? Because she's jealous of Tyler being with her sister?"

"Well, that's what Lucy thought," Emmy said, "But then she realized that she didn't actually know who killed her because all she saw was her dead body on the floor. She was also super drunk that night because you know, they spiked their cups of tea…anyway, she was keen on saying that Bree killed her because it was Bree who found her in the bathroom…then in some of their conversations when she tried to coax Bree to kill Angeline, Bree kept on repeating that she wasn't at fault for killing Lucy. So now, Lucy is confused and wants to know the truth once and for all. It's really complicated because Tyler refuses to talk about her, at least not in a romantic manner…And anyway—"

"Wait," Daniel said, "So, you're saying that somehow, Lucy had a lot to do with Angeline's death, too?"

"Yeah. She did it because she wants to get some revenge."

"And…now she doesn't know who really killed her?"

"Yes. I mean, she got confused and all…"

"And how do you know all these?"

"She's talking to me again, Dan." Emmy said. "I wouldn't want anything to do with this but she's asking me for help. I mean, how could I not help her when I know she badly needs my help? Everyone deserves to know the truth, Dan."

"Em, I get it that you want to help people out but this whole Lucy thing is getting absurd."

"Why?" She asked, "Because she's a ghost?" Even she felt that it was actually absurd but she also couldn't let Lucy down. Not now.

Daniel took a deep breath. "Are you sure that you know what you're doing?"

"Don't you have faith in me, Dan?"

"It's not like that. It's just—"

"Why are you even here this early? Did something happen at work?" Emmy asked as she washed her hands.

"Actually," he said, "I'm here to ask you something."

"Wh-what do you mean?"

"I'm here to ask you to come with me to Alabama."

"Alabama?" She was surprised. "Why?"

"You see, there's this big project at work and our client's from Alabama… It's a pretty nice housing project, you know? And I thought it would be cool if we could stay there for a while. With Wendy, of course. It would be a good experience for us…something new." He smiled.

She smiled back but spoke with a lot of hesitation. "Dan, I'd love to, but…I can't."

"Because of Lucy?"

"Yes." She answered meekly.

"Honey, don't you feel like you're letting Lucy take over your life?"

"But…" Emmy said, "I couldn't just leave her alone, especially now."

For a while, none of them spoke and the air felt heavy and full of unsaid words. Then, Daniel spoke. "Okay," he said, "I'll just be outside."

"Dan," she said, reaching for Daniel's hand. "I'm sorry."

"It's okay." He muttered, but she knew that there wasn't any truth to it.

She watched him walk away from her, feeling like it was the beginning of the end for them.

You can say a lot of things about me, especially because of what you think you know…but somehow, I guess it's still fitting that I tell you that I'm not someone who likes it when others get hurt.

I mean, at least not the people I like.

To be honest, I don't want this to happen to Emmy and Daniel. They're really nice people, but how could I even show myself to Daniel when I know he doesn't believe in me?

It's important to at least believe in something for you to be able to see it, or feel it.

However, in the kind of life that people live these days, it's so hard to make a lot of people believe. It's so hard to actually talk to them, open up their minds, and make them realize that life isn't always in black and white and more often than not, there is more to the things they know about.

The only problem is how.

And right now, I really do not want to think about that.

I just don't want to think about anything at all.

Chapter 23
Cold And Lifeless

Emmy went up to their bedroom and plopped down on the bed. She felt so tired and heartbroken and she didn't know what to do anymore. She was torn between helping Lucy, and going to Alabama with Daniel.

Well, she already made her choice. She knew that she hurt Daniel, but she couldn't live with herself knowing she won't be able to help Lucy. That's not what she wants. She wants to know what really happened and she wants to understand how it all came down to this. She wants to find out the roots of the problem because only then would they all be able to move on.

"I'm sorry." Lucy said as she came floating near Emmy.

Emmy took a deep breath and opened the dresser to find a suitable night gown for her. "It's okay." She told Lucy. "It's not your fault. I mean, I do wish he could see you but what else could I do about that?" She then dressed herself up and fixed her hair. She sat down in front of the dresser and combed her hair. "So," she then said, "Can you tell me about how it felt when you saw yourself…you know, dead?"

"Huh," Lucy expressed, "I don't know about that."

"Luce,"

"Fine, fine," Lucy said. "Well…to be honest, I don't know. I mean, one minute I was sleeping then I felt so hot, you know, because of the alcohol and I wanted to pee and wash my face so I went to the bathroom…then, while I was washing my face, my eyes half closed, someone came in…I'm trying so hard to remember who it was but I don't know. I thought it was Bree, though, because she's fond of showing up just like that and butting into things…then suddenly, I felt some hands on my head and I was being pushed down the faucet, which prompted me to puke. I tried to fight but whoever it was, was just so strong…like that person actually planned for this to happen, or that she just didn't let us all know about what she's capable of.

I remember puking over and over again. I remember being so dizzy that I didn't know how long it lasted for me to actually try to fight whoever it was until the time when I was pushed to my death on the toilet bowl. It seemed all of a sudden that I didn't feel much, except for the fact that I was being suffocated and I don't know how much time passed until Bree found me cold and lifeless on the floor. After that, the rest of the girls came and they all panicked, and they just didn't know what to do.

I didn't know how to feel. I was so mad and sad and I just…I just wanted to be alive." She was crying. "I wanted to stay but I wasn't given the opportunity to. Needless to say, all their lives changed after that moment. They all just drifted apart. Bree still clung on to Tyler for a time but you know…it didn't last long and soon, they broke up. Then, they grew up and he got together with Angeline and me…well, I just stayed as this young girl obviously. And I guess that's the most frustrating part of all these. You know, that I was never given the chance to stay alive and live a full life. It's heartbreaking."

"I'm sorry." Emmy said. "I really am. I know this is hard and it's not the easiest situation to be in but I promise…I'll try my best to help you. Okay? We'll manage."

"Thanks." Lucy said and they shared a smile.

At that moment, Daniel opened the door and went inside the room to find Emmy looking at someone—but the thing is that he couldn't see who or what she's looking at.

"Em?" He announced.

Emmy looked at Daniel and smiled slightly. "Dan," She said, stood up, and gave him a light hug. "I'm sorry, I was just talking to Lucy here—" She said, looking at Lucy who was floating near her.

"Lucy?" Daniel asked. "Honey…there's no one here."

"Can't you see her? She's just right here."

"No." Daniel said, "Honey, no one's here."

Emmy looked at Lucy who was telling her sorry, and looked at Daniel who still couldn't see Lucy.

At that moment, she felt like she didn't know what to believe in anymore.

I remember the very first time I felt invisible.

I was still alive then, just a kid who thought that the world was a bed of roses; a kid who had a lot of dreams; a kid who thought that she was the best thing in her parents' life.

Then one day, while they were enrolling me in school, they talked to the principal as if I wasn't around. They told him that though I looked "nice", which as everyone knows is another word for "not so good looking", and that they thought the school could do a lot to help me harness my skills...they talked about how I was so shy, how they felt like I couldn't relate to others, and how they felt like I could be so much more.

They were talking about me as if I wasn't there.

And, I guess, that's one of the worst things in life: people talking about you like you're not around, not caring about how you'd feel—not caring whether they could hear you or not.

Chapter 24
What The Hell Happened?

(7 years ago)

"AHHHHHHH!!!!!" The sound of Bree's loud screams enveloped the second floor hallway of Libby's house where the rooms were located. Libby's parents weren't around. They were on one of their trips to Cabo and so only the girls were at home.

Bree, Angeline, and Laurel were in one room, while Libby and Lucy were in the other. It was a cold morning, and no one knew that it was the kind of day that would change their lives forever.

"HELP!!!!" Bree called out. "HELP, PLEASE!!! WHERE ARE ALL OF YOU?!"

Libby stirred in her sleep and didn't want to wake up. She straightened out her arms and noticed that Lucy wasn't in the room. Huh, she thought, what time is it? Are they all awake already? And why's Bree shouting?

Oh my god, Bree is shouting! She realized, and tried all her might to get out of the bed fast.

In the other room, Laurel was trying to wake Angeline up. "Hey," she said, "Hey, Anj. Come on. Bree's in the bathroom--"

"What—" Angeline stirred, "It's early—what time is it?"

"7-ish?"

"OH MY GOD!!!!"

Angeline then sat up on the bed and Laurel stopped in her tracks as they heard Libby screaming. "What the hell's going on?!" Laurel asked.

"Come on," Angeline said, got out of bed, and took Laurel's hand and made their way to the bathroom.

Bree was shaking and so was Libby.

Lucy was lying on the floor, her face and hair wet, puke near the toilet and on the faucet. Lucy didn't look like a normal person anymore: her lips were dry, her hands were cold—everything about her was cold and lifeless. In short, she was no longer alive.

"Oh my god," Libby said, with tears in her eyes. "Oh my god, she's not breathing—she's---oh god no—"

"What's going on?" Laurel asked.

"I don't know." Bree answered, her hands shaking, "I was…I wanted to wash my face and pee and when I opened the door, I saw her with her head on the toilet and I…I didn't know what to do," She was crying so hard now that it scared the girls, "I wanted to get her attention and when I touched her, she fell and…oh god what are we gonna do? We'll be in a lot of trouble." She cried some more, which prompted Angeline to hug her.

They were all crying and in a state of panic now.

"We should call the police, right?" Angeline asked. "Or 911 or—"

"Don't you get it?" Libby asked, "We'll be in trouble. I'll be in trouble! You think my parents would—oh god—this is insane. Who would do this?!"

"It's probably an accident." Laurel said, "I mean…you guys were all drunk last night and maybe she had a little too much."

"And she ended up dead." Bree stated. "She shouldn't be dead. I mean…this is just…"

"Are you sure you didn't wake up last night?" Libby asked Bree. "You're fond of taunting her. I mean, maybe you were too drunk and you decided to—"

"What? Kill her?!" Bree said, "Are you insane?!"

"I didn't say that." Libby said. "But, it's just that things between you ended up on a bad note last night and I thought that maybe—"

"Oh don't be insane, Libby." Bree argued, "You're the one who slept in the same room with her! Maybe, this is your fault. Maybe, you put something on her drink or led her to the bathroom and—"

"You're ridiculous! Why would I even think of doing that? I have no anger whatsoever at Lucy, unlike you!"

"Guys, enough—" Angeline said, "No one wanted this to happen."

"How sure are you of that?" Libby asked.

"Guys—" Laurel said, "We can't just leave her here or...let's just call—"

"Libby?"

They were startled when they heard the voice of Libby's mother, Mrs. Amelia Kutcher.

"Oh god, oh god...we're all in trouble—"Libby stammered.

"Libby?" She called out again. "I came back early, your dad's taken a side trip to San Diego. Why the hell is this house trashed? Where are you?" She was then making her way up the stairs and the girls really didn't know what to do. They were just stuck in the bathroom, clinging to the last few moments of their sanity.

"Libby? Why aren't you speaking?" Amelia said as she arrived in the bathroom and opened the door wide. "What's going on—" She stopped when she saw Lucy dead on the floor. "Oh my god!" She called out. "What did you do?!"

"Mom," Libby cried, "It's—it's an accident."

"Oh it better be." Amelia said. "I'll call 911."

They all clung on to hope, for at that moment, that was all they had left.

Fear is a very huge thing.

It's one of those things in life that could cripple you, and make you question everything.

That morning when Libby's mom found my body, I knew that the girls just wanted to do everything they could to turn back time, so they could come to a decision on what they could do with my body, before the police or 911 comes.

But of course, they didn't have much time.

No one really has enough time to begin with, anyway.

They feared for their lives. They feared that everything was going to change. They feared for a lot of things.

And I?

I feared the fact that I would no longer be me. I feared the fact that I would no longer get to live my life, because even if it wasn't the best kind of life—it was still life.

And being alive is still better than being someone who most people could no longer see anymore.

Being alive is more important than anything.

Chapter 25
She Bleeds

Emmy was cooking clam chowder in the kitchen the following afternoon. Wendy was being noisy, because she could smell seafood, and so Emmy was having a hard time multitasking trying to calm Wendy down and making sure the food stayed good. Just then, someone rang the doorbell and Emmy was prompted to turn down the heat of the gas range and see who was out there.

She opened the front door and got a happy surprise when she saw Audrina Naimero, her old friend, outside the door.

"Auee!!!" She greeted and gave her friend a hug.

"Hey, beautiful." Audrina smiled and hugged her back.

"Oh, I'm so happy to see you!" Emmy exclaimed and led her to the kitchen. "You hungry? I'm cooking some clam chowder."

Wendy then purred at Audrina.

"Hey, little pretty!" Audrina greeted Wendy and carried her. "Oh you missed me?" She kissed him on the nose. "You're so big now!"

"She is!" Emmy laughed. "Have to put her on a diet, you know…she just couldn't stop eating!"

"Coz you're her mother!" Audrina grinned. "Who wouldn't want to eat what you serve?"

"Shut it," Emmy quipped. She then turned off the pot, put some food on Wendy's bowl, and prepared some bowls so she and Audrina could eat. Audrina sat down as Emmy handed her a bowl. "I thought I'd cook something nice for Daniel before he goes to Alabama, then I realized that I haven't tried cooking clam chowder before, so…" She took a deep breath and ladled some on Audrina's bowl.

She also took a lemon infused water pitcher from the fridge and poured Audrina a glass.

"Thanks," Audrina said and drank some water after a few spoonfuls of soup. "This soup is amazing," she said, "why didn't I drop by sooner?"

They both laughed.

"So…" Audrina said as Emmy sat down on the chair across Audrina's. "How are you? How are things between you and Dan?"

"Good," Emmy said.

"Really now?" Audrina asked, raising an eyebrow.

Emmy sighed. "I don't know, Au," She said, "Things have been crazy recently."

"Right." Audrina said. "Like, you were involved in that imprisonment of that Bree girl who killed her sister, like you're this town's sleuth again."

"Yeah, well…"

"You know, you're amazing and all that, but why do you keep propping up on these situations…" Audrina took a deep breath. "It's not that I could blame you, I mean, you were only trying to help, but your dad got worried. I did, too."

"You didn't have to." Emmy answered. "How's dad?"

"Oh, he's good." Audrina smiled, probably thinking of Troy Byrne, Emmy's father and her boyfriend. "He's actually planning to go on a trip to Maldives. I mean, with me. You and Dan should come, too! After his Alabama trip, of course, but—"

"I'd love to," Emmy said, "Maldives is amazing but…I just don't think I could right now. I mean, there are things I have to fix—"

"Like, that ghost who's trying to ask you for help?"

"Audrina, she has a name and it's Lucy. She's annoying, yes, but I couldn't just let her down. I mean, she died not knowing who killed her. The least I could do is make sure that her soul finally gets to rest in peace if she finally knows who did this to her, you know? I can't just be the kind of person who lets this case go just because no one else could see my client, if that's what you want to call her."

"Listen," Audrina said, "I cannot see ghosts right now, and I couldn't see this Lucy but that doesn't mean I don't believe you, okay?" She said. "I've had a brush with these things before...back when my papa, my grandpa, died... He would often show me signs that he's around by blowing wind in the room when it's extremely hot, or letting butterflies fly around the room when it's raining outside...then one day, I got to talk to him with the help of a friend of mine. Her name's Cassiopeia and she's always had this gift of talking to ghosts. Actually, she's living here in Sky Valley now, so you know..." She took a deep breath. "Anyway, all I want you to know is that even though you think I don't care, I do. I just don't want you to sabotage your relationship with Daniel all because of helping a ghost."

"So...you don't want me to help her?"

"Well, that's really up to you." Audrina said. "I just don't want you to get all caught up in this...but I know it's really hard not to get caught up in this so... why don't we just watch some TV?"

Emmy laughed. For some reason, she found this to be comforting; that no matter how crazy life was right now, at least, Audrina was there for her and she'll be able to get through this.

"I think I'd like that." She smiled.

"Come on then." Audrina smiled back.

The first time that I came across another ghost was when I was newly dead, excuse the term.

I was floating around my old room, which my parents were already trying so hard to redecorate or bulldoze out of the house altogether, when this ghost named Mia came inside the room and introduced herself as someone who used to live in the house next to ours. She said she died because she was born with a heart condition and when she turned sixteen, this heart condition got the best of her and so she died.

I really didn't want to talk to her. I mean, I had nothing to do with her, I didn't know her, and obviously, it felt stupid thinking that she might be able to help me out in some way.

Turns out, she only wanted to have someone to talk to. I guess ghosts could get a lot lonelier than usual, too.

We became friends for…I really don't know how long as I've told you that time is kind of crazy when it comes to us ghosts, but anyway…she was my best friend for a long time until she realized that she had no more business here and that she was finally okay with being dead.

So, she left and here I am, still alone, still such a loser—even as a ghost.

To be honest, I guess I'm just scared of going…I don't know where once all this is done.

I'm still scared.

Some things just don't change.

Chapter 26
She's A Bitch

The Sky Valley Prison is one of the worst places on earth, Emmy thought.

Of course, she never had a thing for jails (who would?), and she didn't want to be reminded of Lena McMahon anymore, but if there's something she's learned the past couple of days, it's the fact that you can never really let go of your past completely. There are times when you have to come to terms with it again so you could finally let go.

Today, she was going to see Bree in hopes that she could coax some information out of her to give light to everything that's happened.

Bree was escorted by some female guards and allowed her to sit across Emmy. Emmy thanked the guards and they stayed in a position that's not too near—or too far—from Emmy and Bree.

"What do you want?" Bree asked. "I thought the show's over."

Emmy took a deep breath. "There are just some things I am confused about. Like…your connection to Lucy's death."

"I told you I didn't kill her. But whatever," Bree scoffed, "No one believes me, anyway."

"Look," Emmy said, "the thing is…I believe you."

"What?" Bree asked, surprised. "What do you mean?"

"I know that I don't know you or your past, but recent events helped me realize that things aren't always as they seem…and Lucy—"

"Lucy." Bree repeated and looked at Emmy, "What has she got to do with this? Wait…Don't tell me you could hear her, too?"

"No, uhm…I couldn't just hear her, I can also see her."

"See her? Like, as a ghost?"

"Yep."

"Are you kidding me?"

"No, I'm not." Emmy answered. "That's also the reason why I got involved in this case before. Lucy showed herself up to me and asked me to help her. So...I'm here."

"But you also thought that I killed her, right? Isn't that what she always used to say?"

"Yes," Emmy answered, "but then she realized that maybe, it's not you. Well, she...she realized that she didn't see the face of the person who killed her so she really doesn't know who killed her. She just always thought that it's you because you really hated her before and you always had issues with her so..."

"The idiot." Bree declared. "She ruined my life!"

"Well, in case you've forgotten, Bree, you did kill Angeline, you know."

"Yeah, but that's because Lucy kept on telling me to do so! She played with my brain. She's wicked. And you know what? If that's her idea of revenge then maybe, you should think about backing out of helping her because she's just insane, okay? She'll take revenge on you, too."

"I'm not doing anything wrong, Bree." Emmy said, "And besides, you can't expect me to just drop this case altogether. You hated her, she thought you killed her—"

"So she asked me to kill someone else in the process?"

Emmy took a deep breath. "You wouldn't have killed Angeline if you also didn't harbor ill feelings against her."

"Angeline's always brought up as the good one while I'm always played as the rotten egg! How do you think I feel about that, huh? And, yeah, fine, I admit that I did listen to Lucy but...but I also regret what I did. Angeline's my sister, even though we didn't always see eye to eye, you know what I mean? It's not that I hated her, it's just that...she almost always got what she wanted and Tyler was the last straw. Lucy also hated me because she felt like I took her parents away from her so...I guess, we both got what we wanted, just not in the way we expected."

For a couple of seconds, not one of them spoke. It was a heavy moment and Emmy was still coming to terms as to how she could deal with it. It wasn't a very nice thing to be part of, and for that, she hated herself.

Then, finally, Bree found the courage to speak again.

"You should also talk to Laurel Hamilton and Libby Lopez, you know? Find out what you can. Because if Lucy has been telling you the truth, then you also probably know by now that I wasn't the only person with her in that house. I'm not the only one who's capable of being guilty. I hope you haven't forgotten that."

Anger can turn your life around—for the better, or for the worse.

There are times when anger motivates you to be better than the person you are; to work harder to prove who everyone who put you down wrong; to show people who never had faith in you that you could actually rise, and that you could achieve the things you want without their help.

But there are also times when anger could drive you mad and maim you in such a way that you become someone you never thought you could be; someone who's so mad at the world that she doesn't know how to go forth with her day without hurting anyone; someone who uses anger to hurt and manipulate people; someone who uses anger for revenge.

Revenge could be a tricky thing.

Some days, you think that after you have pulled your revenge on someone, it already means that you're amazing, and that you finally got what you want. What most people forget to tell you is that revenge, just like anger, is a two-edged sword: it makes you happy, but at the same time, it also pierces you and drills a hole in your heart that you never know how to heal.

A wound that you don't know could still be healed.

And for that, revenge means almost nothing.

Why bother?

Why not?

Chapter 27
What Have You Done?

"How was it?" Lucy asked Emmy as she came inside the bedroom that day, after visiting Bree in jail. "What did she tell you?"

"That she didn't kill you." Emmy said as she removed her pearl earrings, formerly owned by her mother, and placed them in a box in the drawer. "She said that you tricked her into killing Angeline, but I also told her that if she didn't harbor any ill feelings against Angeline at all, then she wouldn't have killed her."

"Right."

"But you know, that doesn't make you any less guilty."

"I know." Lucy answered.

"And you know what?" Emmy asked. "I'm beginning to think that the reason why you really wanted me to believe that Bree is at fault is because you hated her with a passion."

"I'm not denying that."

"Luce, anger could make you do the worst things." She said. "It could make you trick people into believing things that they really shouldn't believe in." She then took her laptop from the bed and turned it on.

"I know that," Lucy said, "and I'm sorry, okay? That's why I'm trying to undo my mistakes. Anyway, what else did she say?"

"She told me to talk to Laurel and Libby." Emmy answered, "She also told me that because she wasn't the only person with you that day, then you really couldn't say that she's guilty. And I guess, in a way, she's right." Emmy looked at Lucy. "Listen," she told her, "Why didn't you ever tell me before about Laurel and Libby maybe being guilty, too?"

Lucy swooped around her and spoke. "Like I said," she said, "I was really angry at Bree and I thought that all her pent up anger for me from years ago were enough reason for her to kill me. She was…she's the kind of person who could do that, you know? I felt like she had it in her. Libby, though she could be bitchy, too, was just…she was a little too cowardly for this. I would never think that she could do it, but from the way things are, she could be a suspect, too. Laurel…she's just too nice, okay? She's smart, and had the right amount of sass and she's intelligent and…and she was like our mother hen. She and Angeline were like the most mature out of us all, and that's why we all looked up to her. I don't think she has any motive…" She then looked at Emmy's laptop. "What's a photo of Laurel doing there?"

"Is this her?" Emmy asked Lucy.

"Yeah."

"I thought her name was Laurel Hamilton…Why's she using the name Laurel Wood?"

"That's her mother's maiden name." Lucy answered. "I don't know…maybe, she wanted to get away from the memory of what happened 7 years ago and she thought that changing her surname would do her good. What does she do now? Is that like, a blog?"

"Uh-huh." Emmy answered. "She has a cooking blog. Seems to have a pretty decent following, too."

"She was always such a good cook even at a young age."

Emmy took a deep breath, opened another tab and typed "Libby Lopez Sky Valley Georgia" in the search bar. Almost no results came up, except for a Facebook Page of one Libby Lopez, a woman in her 20's with brunette locks cut to her shoulder, and cat eyes (she's obviously a fan of the cat-eyeliner look). Emmy also noticed that she now lives in Mountain Valley, Sky Valley's neighboring town.

"That's Libby now? Wow." Lucy said. "I forgot to tell you that she no longer lives here."

"Yeah, apparently, she's already residing in Mountain Valley."

"Mountain Valley, wow." Lucy said. "Isn't flight a sign of guilt?"

"Luce, you can't always generalize things."

"But—"

Just then, Emmy's phone rang and she found that it was Daniel on the other end of the line.

"How are you?" Daniel asked.

"I'm alright, how are you? Not stressing yourself too much?"

"No. You?"

"I'm fine, Dan."

"Listen," Daniel said. "I know I left on a not so good note but I want you to know that I love you, okay? See you when I get back?"

"Of course." Emmy replied and found herself smiling lightly. "I love you, too."

The call ended and Emmy realized that she needed to talk to someone. She took a deep breath, dialed Audrina's number and spoke.

"Audrina," She said as Audrina picked up, "I need your help."

There are some people who'll be willing to do what they could to help you. There are some people who will make you realize that you do not need the entire world—as long as you have the best people at hand.

And that's one of those things in life that you have to be thankful for. If you don't have these people around you, you probably won't be able to get what you really want.

I wish I had friends like that when I was alive.

I thought I had, but then again, life could trick you into believing things that you really shouldn't believe in.

I guess, it's always up to you how you want to deal with things and think about what life really is about.

That's the age-old question, I guess, and no one really knows what the right answer is. And somehow, that makes things all the more complicated.

And complicated isn't always good.

Chapter 28
Laurel And Libby

"Is this the right way?" Audrina asked Emmy while they were in her car that day, going to Laurel's house so Emmy could talk to her.

"Yeah, I believe it's this." Emmy answered. "Cherry Street is right there so—"

"What do you think of that Libby girl living in Mountain Valley now?"

"I don't know, Au," Emmy answered. "I mean, maybe she has her reasons. Maybe, it's too painful to be here, but then again, that's an obvious sign of flight. But...in cases like this, it's just so hard to make a conclusion."

"Especially because your dear client is a ghost."

"Au,"

"Hello? I'm here." Lucy said from behind them. "And look, we're here. This is Laurel's house." She said and thought that not much has changed about Laurel's house. It was still the same house that she remembered from when they were kids—white, with a white picket fence, and flowers in front. In short, it was a pristine house; a house that will make you think that the person living there is clean and pure and couldn't think about bad things about others.

"This is her house?" Emmy asked.

"Yeah," Lucy answered.

"Come on."

They then made their way out of the car and Emmy took the responsibility of ringing the doorbell. For a couple of seconds, no one came out of the house.

"Maybe she isn't here." Audrina answered.

"She is! I could feel her!" Lucy said a little too loudly.

"Okay, okay," Audrina said, "I can hear you, you know?"

Emmy rolled her eyes, rang the doorbell again, and then waited for Laurel. And then after a few seconds, someone opened the door. Emmy thought that this woman was beautiful: She had layered brown hair, and was wearing square-rimmed eyeglasses that made her look kind, gentle, and smart. She definitely looked like she did on her blog.

"Yes?" Laurel said. "Can I help you?"

"Uhm, Hi. Laurel Wood, right?" Emmy asked.

"Yes, that's me." Laurel smiled. "How may I help you?"

"Hi," Emmy said and shook Laurel's hand. "I've been reading your blog and I thought I could see you for an interview. I know it's on short notice but...I hope you don't mind."

"Uhm, yeah," Laurel said, with a hint of hesitation in her voice. She then looked at Emmy and Audrina and smiled. "Yeah, sure, come in."

She led them to the den and told them to wait for her there.

"She has a big house..." Audrina quipped, as she looked at the number of antiques in the den. There were a number of pictures lining the walls, too - pictures of Laurel as a kid, of her during her High School Graduation, of her family, and of an adult Laurel. Emmy thought that she had a lot of pain in her eyes.

"Yeah, they're very rich." Lucy said.

"She really couldn't see you?"

"If she could, she probably wouldn't have let you in."

Emmy and Audrina sat down on the couch just as Laurel came back in the den. "I've some fresh watermelon juice and green tea cookies. Would you be okay with this?"

"Oh, it's more than enough." Emmy smiled.

"So…" Laurel said, "What did you want to talk to me about?"

"Uhm, I've been reading your blog," Emmy said, "And I thought that you really are a skilled food photographer. So, where do you get your inspiration?"

"Oh, uhm…I've always loved cooking. I've been cooking since I was a kid and I thought if I could turn it into something that could inspire others, then why not, right? So…that's it, I thought I'd put up a blog and I did."

"Those macaroons look divine!"

"But you make them, too, right?" Laurel asked. "I mean, you're Emmy Byrne, right?" She said. "I know who you are, Emmy." Her demeanor suddenly changed. "And…if I were you, I'd say what's going on right now before I even think of asking you and your friend to get the hell out of my house."

Emmy took a deep breath. She wasn't expecting this. "Look," she said, "I'm just here to ask you about what you know about Lucy's death, you know, 7 years ago, since you were friends and all—"

"I don't know what you're trying to do, Emmy," Laurel said, "but you have to know that I've moved past that point in my life. It's already traumatic as it is. I lost one of my best friends so I hope you understand that I really do not want to talk about it. It was an accident."

"But do you seriously believe that?"

Laurel took a deep breath. "As far as I'm concerned, Emmy, I'm not the one you should be asking all these questions. I'm not the one who's in jail. I'm also not the one who's living in Mountain Valley because she's so scared of being in the town where her best friend died." She said. "So, who's guilty now?"

There are times in life when you could be guilty about things you really shouldn't be guilty about.

But you know what's wrong about most people?

They feel guilty about things they have nothing to do with, but they become defensive about things they really should be guilty about.

As you can see, humans are very complicated. They never say what they mean, and they never mean what they say. This of course causes a lot of pain and confusion for everyone around them. But, they don't even feel guilty about it because they think they're just doing the right thing.

The right thing for them, but not for everyone else.

The right thing for them—and that's why they choose to continue with this "right thing", instead of actually finding out the truth, and allowing their guilt to consume them, so people who need to be freed could be freed.

But you know what?

That's the thing about people: they're all naturally selfish—and they don't even want to recognize it.

Chapter 29
A Trip To Mountain Valley

"So, we just go round the corner and drive to that house by the fountain, is that right?" Audrina asked her friend, Mia, who's from Mountain Valley. She and Emmy were on a quest to find Libby in Mountain Valley the following day, after their crazy encounter with Laurel yesterday. "Alright, thanks." Audrina said and shut her phone down.

"She says we just have to find the fountain." She told Emmy who was then driving. Emmy drove the car around the corner of a street named Grande, and there they found a fountain featuring two angels and a woman, possibly patterned from Venus De Milo in the middle. Near the fountain stood an old, baroque-style house. It was flanked by Rhododendron trees, roses on the ground, and brick walls.

"Is that it?" Emmy asked Audrina.

"I think that's it." Lucy answered.

"Yeah, maybe that's it." Audrina added.

They then went out of the car. If only they weren't there to investigate about Lucy's death, they'd both think that it was a good day. The sky was overcast, there were pigeons flying and pecking on seeds on the ground, and there were a few people walking in peace. It seemed like the perfect town to hide in, though, because there weren't a lot of people around and no one would think that someone who was once so lively, so bitchy, and so full of energy would live in such a solemn place.

"What are you guys waiting for?!" Lucy told them.

Audrina rolled her eyes, "Easy, Lucy."

They then walked to the house and Emmy knocked on the door. She thought the door was beautiful and was intricately made. After three knocks, they waited for someone to open the door and soon enough, Libby was right there in front of them. She had her hair in a ponytail and she was wearing an over-sized shirt and denim shorts. "Yes?" She said.

"Hi, you're Libby Lopez, right?" Emmy asked.

"Yes, that's me. What can I do for you?"

"Uhm…we just want to ask you some questions about your friend Bree."

Libby stopped and looked at them with a lot of suspicion in her eyes. "She's not my friend." She said, and everyone noticed how her voice quivered. "Now, if you don't mind, I have a lot to do so—"

"Why are you acting like you're a guilty person?" Audrina raised her eye-brow. "We just want to ask you some questions. There is nothing wrong with that. We don't have the police with us. We're not armed. You can search our car. Although we do have this ghost with us—"

"Ghost?"

"Audrina!" Emmy said then turned to Libby again. "Look, we know Bree. Not for a long time but we've spent some time with her lately and…well, in case you still didn't know, she's involved in the murder of your friend, Angeline."

"I know that." Libby muttered. "Can't say I was surprised considering she probably also killed Lucy."

"See, that's the thing." Emmy said, "Lucy thinks that Bree didn't kill her. And that's why we're here."

"Are you insane?" Libby scoffed. "Lucy's dead. You couldn't have talked to her."

"Except she talks to us." Emmy said. "Look, long story short, this thing still has a lot of loopholes and it would be tremendously helpful if you'd tell us what you really know."

"Are you fucking kidding me?"

"Tell her Don got married just last week. And he finally was able to throw away all her stuff from when they were together, especially that bear she so loved." Lucy said.

"Lucy says that your ex, Don, finally got married last week and was able to throw away everything you ever shared, especially that bear that was really special to you." Emmy said.

"Oh my god, how on earth do you even know that?" Libby asked, confused. She then shook her head. "I don't know how you know that but…" She sighed. "Come in." She led them into the house and closed the door behind them. "You couldn't stay long, okay?" She stated. "Just tell me what you want to know."

"Nice house." Audrina quipped.

Emmy rolled her eyes then spoke. "Look, we just want to know what really happened the morning that Lucy died."

"I already told you, none of this was my fault." Libby said. "You think I'd kill her? Sure, I loved taunting her and all that but I am not a fucking killer. I lost everything when she died, you know? My parents had me transferred to another school; they wouldn't allow me to go out…I had to break up with Don. I had to leave everyone, everything…and after college, I decided to just leave Sky Valley altogether. I couldn't stay there anymore. It was just too much."

"But weren't you in the same room with her just hours before she died?"

"Yeah, but I was sleeping. I've always been a tight sleeper and besides, we had our drinks spiked that day."

"Which of course was your idea, right?"

"Yeah, but that has nothing to do with what happened to her. It's unfortunate, I know, and it has haunted me all my life but…I swear, I didn't kill her."

"But Laurel said that you're here because you're guilty?"

"She said that?" Libby asked and shook her head. "What will you get out of this? Lucy's dead. No one was able to figure out what happened to her so why bother?"

"We just want to help her out."

"So you really want me to believe that she's here right now?"

"She really is here."

"Oh, you have got to be kidding me."

Sometimes, it's so hard to make people see and recognize you because they refuse to. They do not want to believe that you're around so they decide that you're just not there and that you don't belong with them.

The thing with people is that if you come into a room so quietly, they don't bother to see you. But, if you come with a lot of violence, with a lot of presence, they realize that you're there. You see, people often don't like what's quiet and easy; they want the grand gestures. They want to see before they believe—even if they already know the truth in their hearts.

People do not trust easily—but when they do, they could be wrong. When they do, they could be maligned; mistreated; misjudged.

People only trust when there's a big blast of trust, of hope, that's given unto them. Otherwise, they could all just be a bunch of idiots.

Idiots who have no idea who they are or what's going on in the world that they're living in anymore.

Chapter 30
I Know What To Do

Libby laughed. "Excuse me, but I am already old enough not to believe in ghosts and fairy tales and—"

"Just because you cannot see something doesn't mean that it isn't true." Emmy said. "Maybe, you can't see her because you've forgotten her. You couldn't see her because you chose to forget her and try to move on with your life."

"Tell her that if she still refuses to believe that I'm here, I'll do something evil."

Emmy took a deep breath. "Lucy says that she'll do something evil if you still wouldn't believe that she's here."

"Oh yeah?" Libby challenged. "Try me."

Just then, the lights in the living room flickered and the vase that was resting on the center table fell down the floor. The cabinets shook as if there was an earthquake, and the trinkets that Libby kept there also fell down the floor.

"Lucy, stop!" Emmy said.

"Oh my god—" Libby said as she held on to the wall. "Okay, fine!" She said.

"Fine! I believe in you now, Lucy! Why don't you show yourself to me?!"

"It's not that simple." Emmy said. "You've refused to see her for so long that she could no longer show herself to you."

"But how could I help her if I couldn't even see her?"

"Well—"

"I have an idea. I think I know what to do." Audrina said.

"What is it?" Emmy and Libby asked at the same time.

"Em, remember this psychic friend I'm telling you about? She still lives in Sky Valley. I think she could help us. What do you think?"

"Oh no, I won't ever go back to Sky Valley." Libby said.

"What are you so scared of?" Emmy asked. "Do you want to help Lucy or not? And besides, if you have nothing to be guilty of then why would you even be scared?"

Libby sighed. "Fine." She said. "But Laurel has to come, too."

"Of course". Emmy said, although she was unsure of it. "We'll see her later." Libby took a deep breath. "Fine. You can go now."

"Oh no, young lady." Audrina said. "You're coming with us. We can't just let you stay here. Besides, it wouldn't be for long. After this whole commotion is over, you can go back here."

"You're kidding, right?"

"Think of this as the last thing you'd ever do for Lucy." Emmy told Libby. "Or, maybe you want her to create a mess in here again—"

"Fine, fine." Libby sighed. "Oh, you guys are crazy!" She said. "Fine, I'm coming with you."

"Good." Audrina quipped.

***

Emmy rang the doorbell of Laurel's house later that day after their trip to Mountain Valley. Audrina and Libby were at Emmy's house.

Laurel came out after a couple of seconds. "You again." She said when she saw Emmy. "I told you I have nothing to do about Lucy and all that shit." She said, looking way more stressed than she did yesterday. "What are you doing here?"

"Well, we got your friend Libby to come with us."

"Come? Here?"

"Yep." Emmy answered. "You can see her tomorrow. Come with us, we'll be seeing a psychic. You know, to finally put your questions about Lucy to rest."

"I have no questions about Lucy because she's killed by either Bree or Libby. Not me. You could ask her, if you could really see her. I've never been anything but nice to her all her life. I was a friend to her when none of them was."

"Well, she says that if you're still really her friend then you'd be willing to help us out."

Laurel took a deep breath. "Look, I did everything I could for her when she was still alive. I did everything to save her...you know, so she wouldn't feel so bad about herself and about this unfair shit of a world. I think it would be best if you'd just leave me alone. Talk to that psychic if you want to, but I also advice that you go see a shrink because you're all going crazy. And if you ask me one more time, I'll call the cops." She then went back inside the house and slammed the door.

Emmy took a deep breath. "That didn't go well." She said and noticed that Lucy was sad. They were on the way to the car and Lucy looked extremely lonely—the kind of lonely that Emmy hasn't seen before.

"Hey," She told Lucy as they entered the car. "It's all going to be fine." She said. "Believe me, it's gonna be fine. We'll figure this out."

"I hope so." Lucy said. "Oh, I do hope so."

For the most part, I wasn't the kid who put out a lot of tantrums and who wanted everything to go her way. Obviously, I didn't have a lot of things going my way, and I guess you know that by now.

Anyway, I remember one of those times when I threw a tantrum. I was twelve and we were supposed to go to the mall and hang out at a friend's house afterwards. My parents allowed Bree and Angeline to join but they told me to just stay at home because I don't have anything to do at the mall.

I felt that it was so unfair because not only will Bree tease me about it later, it's also a sign that they didn't trust me. I screamed and shouted and wanted to let them know that I was there; that I was their daughter and they have to trust me because I wouldn't do anything wrong but instead, they said that they were only protecting me.

From what? I have no idea. I felt like they were only trying to protect themselves.

You see, when you keep someone so sheltered and try to protect her from things she could actually protect herself about, you also tend to ruin her life.

Your parents could do a lot for you, but at the same time, they also could break your heart and turn your life into something that you wouldn't want it to be.

And that sucks.

That always sucks.

Chapter 31
Enter Cassiopeia

"I knew it, I shouldn't have trusted you." Libby said while she, Emmy, Audrina, and Lucy were on the car on the way to Cassiopeia's house. "You said Laurel will be here!"

"Could you please stop bitching?" Audrina asked. "It's not our fault that she didn't want to be here. And you know what? We can figure this out either way. Now, I'm thinking that she had a lot to do with this."

"But she was so nice…" Lucy muttered.

"Nice can be deadly." Emmy said as she turned to a curve. "Nice can be deceiving."

"Look, this is really creepy, okay?" Libby said. "You're like, talking to yourselves."

"Shut up." Emmy and Audrina told Libby.

"That's her house." Audrina told Emmy as they found this purple colored house by the corner of Lemon Street.

"That looks so weird!" Libby said. "Look at that."

"I said shut up." Audrina said.

"Come on." Emmy said and got out of the car and let Audrina help Libby out.

"I'm not a baby, okay?" Libby said. "And I'm not like gonna escape. We're already here and wow…she's a medium, right? Like, I can talk to Lucy through her?"

Audrina rolled her eyes, sighed, and rang the doorbell. They waited for a couple of seconds, all fidgety and confused. It has been quite a stressful few days and they all just want it to end.

Soon, a long-haired woman wearing crescent moon and star-shaped chandelier earrings opened the door. She was also wearing a lime green pashmina, and a flowy white skirt. "Audrina?" She said. "What are you doing here?"

"Cassiopeia." Audrina greeted and gave Cassiopeia a hug. "It's been a while. These are my friends Emmy and Libby, and—"

"You have a ghost in your midst. A girl. Possibly seventeen—"

They all looked at each other, then Audrina spoke. "Exactly." She said. "That's what we came here for. We need your help, Cassiopeia. You see, Emmy and I could hear her, but her friend Libby here cannot. We thought maybe you could help us, you know, so Lucy could talk to Libby."

Cassiopeia took a deep breath. "This isn't easy, Audrina." She said. "I've tried hard not to use my powers anymore because not a lot of people believe in me and…it's just crazy but…but the ghost in your midst has a lot of negative energy in her. She does need help." She took another deep breath and spoke. "Come in."

She led them to the house. It was quite small, Emmy thought, and there were a lot of crystal balls on the shelves. There were also tarot card paintings and a whole lot of curtains. Cassiopeia came back into the room with two red candles and one large white candle. She lit them and asked them to sit in a circle by the round table and hold each other's hands.

"Do not break the circle, especially as I enter into my trance." Cassiopeia said. "It is important."

Emmy was holding Libby's hand and she noticed that it was shaking. Most of them were cold though the room was hot. Then suddenly, a different kind of cold enveloped the room and made them fidget in their seats. It was scary, and unusual.

"Libby." Cassiopeia said, but her voice was different. It was raspy, and it seemed like it was coming from way deep within her, like Lucy was finally inside her. "Olivia Antoinette Lopez."

"Lu—Lucy?" Libby asked, her voice quivering.

"Finally. We had to go through all these just so you'd be able to notice me.

Tell me what you know, Libby. Tell me what you know right away or I will ruin you."

Libby cried. She was extremely frightened. "Lucy, please. I had nothing to do with this. I knew I wasn't the perfect friend but…but I didn't do this. When I woke up that day, you were no longer there. When I woke up, they were all in the bathroom and—"

"But why did you leave Sky Valley? Why?!"

"I was just so scared, Luce. I knew something went wrong, something went awfully wrong that…that led to your death, but Lena McMahon was stupid she didn't even figure it out. Luce, I didn't kill you. I don't know who did but believe me, I've wanted to know who for so long. I just couldn't stay in Sky Valley anymore because of all those crazy memories. I could no longer be there. I'm sorry. I'm so sorry."

She cried, still holding on to Emmy so the circle wouldn't be broken.

Just then Cassiopeia coughed. It was as if Lucy was no longer with her. She looked at all of them and spoke. "She has a lot of pain within her, pain that was able to engulf me. She couldn't see past the pain; she has a lot of blinders on and that's why she couldn't remember who killed her. But I learned something," she said, "Whoever killed her was jealous of her."

"Jealous?" Emmy asked. "What for?"

"The killer was jealous because of how a man named Tyler, the boy Lucy loved all her life, treated her. The killer also had strong feelings for Tyler and she couldn't stomach the fact that Tyler kissed Lucy a couple of hours before she died. She saw them kissing by the bushes. She saw them with her own eyes, and anger—a lot of anger—welled up inside her and she decided that it was time to end Lucy's life once and for all."

They all looked at one another and felt even more confused. What does this all mean? Does this mean that Bree actually had something to do with this? Was she just trolling them all along?

"I need you to do something for me." Cassiopeia said. "I need you to bring Tyler here. I need to see him. I need to talk to him. That will help us get a lot of clarity about this so Lucy could finally be at peace. Please, bring him here."

The closer you are to finding out the truth, the more fearful you could get.

Why?

Because sometimes, it's so hard to actually face the truth. It's hard to be given answers and know that you've been wrong all along.

If you're right, then it would be fine. But what if you're wrong? What if, you actually aided in the destruction of a lot of things in order to find out the truth that has been hidden from you for so long?

Finding out the truth is a very tricky thing. Again, it is never in black and white. It could hurt you. It could make you feel like you're no longer the person you are, and that you have no idea who the person you're about to become is.

It scares you.

It makes you want to hide.

It wants you to go right back to the start.

Chapter 32
Hey Jealousy

"Emmy?" Tyler said as he opened the door. It was obvious that he has seen better days and that he also has been under a lot of stress recently. "What are you doing here?"

"Tyler," Emmy said, "You have to come with us."

"Come where?"

"To Cassiopeia's house."

"What? Who is this?" He asked, his face full of confusion. "What is this about?"

"Hi," Audrina said, "I know you don't know me but I'm here to help out. Cassiopeia's my friend. She's a psychic and she wants to talk to you so we could all find out the truth about what really happened on that night that Lucy died."

"A psychic?" Tyler repeated, even more confused. "Look, Emmy, please just…just let me be in peace. This has dragged on for too long. I don't want anything to do with this anymore."

"Well, neither do I, Tyler." Libby said, appearing from behind them.

"Libby?" Tyler greeted. "You're—you're here."

"Believe me, I didn't want to be here." She said. "But I had to. I knew I had to help Lucy for the last time because no matter how we try to deny it, we're still a part of what happened to her. She's dead because none of us wanted to stick up for her. She's dead because someone hated her too much and we all just believed that it would be better to just let her go and all that, let it all go because it was the easy thing to do. It was the easiest thing to do because we all wanted to escape but then again…how much more could we escape, Tyler? How much more could we make ourselves believe that we had nothing to do with this? Every action has a consequence, and this is our consequence." She went on. "I got to talk to Lucy through Cassiopeia." She had tears in her eyes now. "She…she was so mad, so mad because none of us wanted to help her. She was so mad because she didn't know who killed her. We weren't good to her when she was around—"

"That's not true. I loved her."

None of them could speak for a couple of seconds until Emmy decided to go on.

"Exactly. You loved her." Emmy said. "So why not try to help her? Cassiopeia said that she needs to see you. You need to be there. It will finally make things clear. Please, for the sake of Lucy's soul, please help us."

Tyler and Libby looked at each other and Libby nodded her head.

Tyler took a deep breath and spoke through the tears. "Okay," He said, "Okay."

They then made their way to Emmy's car and drove to Cassiopeia's house.

***

The room was dark and the air was cold. They were in a circle, holding hands, candles in the middle, Cassiopeia looking at Tyler.

"Look at me." Cassiopeia told Tyler. "Look me in the eyes." She said. "Are you ready?"

"Yes." Tyler muttered.

Then everything was different and nothing was ever the same again.

This is it.

This is the final straw before the truth finally shows itself and before every-thing could finally change.

It's funny, you know?

It's like the truth has its own mind; it doesn't want to show itself up right away because it wants you to figure things out for yourself. This way, you'd finally be able to know what you want to know without being spoon-fed.

Because, more often than not, the truth is already there, right in front of our eyes, but we do not want to see it for reasons known only to ourselves.

Chapter 33
The Kiss That Ruined It All

(7 years ago)

It was a hot, sweltering afternoon and Lucy felt that her ruffled yellow taffeta dress was already so hot and so unflattering that it made her look like a cupcake. She didn't even know why she agreed to be in this tea party, except for the fact that her mother's one of the organizers and it would be such a shame if she wouldn't be there.

She was already so tired and she really didn't want to spend much time with Bree and all her friends because she was tired of their banter. She was tired of being with them, period.

Truth be told, there was only one person she wanted to spend time with, but it's been too long since they had time alone, and it's not like she could still be with him because he had a girlfriend. And that girl is Bree, her cousin.

Lucy took a deep breath and tried to drown her sorrows in the tea that Libby spiked earlier. She drank as much as she could, trying to calm her stomach down because she really wasn't a big drinker. Oh boy, she couldn't stomach the scent of chardonnay—it was just too much.

"You really shouldn't be drinking alone, you know?" Tyler said from behind her. Apparently, he found her by the bushes and decided to sit down with her, never mind if their clothes got dirty. He also didn't want to be surrounded by everyone anymore and truth be told, he also didn't want to spend time with Bree. She could be too bitchy and she really wasn't his type.

Sometimes, he hated himself for ever trying to get Bree's attention and making her fall in love with him because he knew how wrong it was. It wasn't the best thing he had done in his life and he was ashamed of it. He actually wanted to be with Lucy, but she stopped talking to him ages ago, and he still didn't know why.

Lucy looked at Tyler who had a hip flask in his hand. "What are you doing here?" She asked.

"I don't know," he said, "Maybe, I want to be alone, too."

"Go somewhere else."

"Why are you so mad at me? What did I do to you?"

Lucy took a deep breath and drank some more tea. She noticed the roses swaying through the wind. "I don't think we should talk about that."

"No, really, why? Because as far as I'm concerned, I did nothing wrong to you. In fact, after that kiss on your 12th birthday, I wanted things to be better between us, to be a couple and all that, but you just disappeared. Why?"

"It's none of your business."

"Really? Because I love you. You know that? I love you and all I've done these past couple of years is try to be close to you again, even having a relationship with Bree in the process. I know it's wrong but…oh whatever!" He then let Lucy face him and kissed her so passionately on the lips. She pulled back at first but decided to let go of all her inhibitions; this was what she always wanted, anyway, and it's finally happening. The kisses were soft, beautiful…they were everything she ever dreamed of and more.

"I love you, Luce."

"I love you, too." She said. "But this isn't right. I don't want Bree to get hurt."

"She'll be okay. I'll end things right now. I'll end things and sure, she'll get mad, but she'll move past it. Your cousin's tough. I don't want to hurt her anymore by pretending that I'm in love with her when I'm really not. I don't want this craziness to continue anymore. I want to make things right."

"But---but she'll hate me. She'll hate us."

"She won't hate you, Luce." He said. "No one saw us kiss. It will be okay."

"You'll really break up with her?"

"Yes." He said. "I'll do anything for you. I'll do anything for us."

"Oh, Tyler." She said and hugged him. They stayed like that for a little while, thinking that no one saw them and that they were safe. They thought they had the whole world in their hands and that they'd finally get whatever it is that they're hoping for, but the truth is far stranger than that.

Because the truth is that someone was watching them and that someone saw the way they kissed. That someone heard about what they were talking about.

And that someone was so mad right now; so mad that she's able to forget who she was; so mad that she allowed her anger to take over her to make her do the unthinkable.

Whenever I think about that kiss, I think about stars and sparkles and all those beautiful things.

I think about how much hope I had in my heart then, and how I thought that everything would finally be right in the world—in my world.

I thought about how love was actually real and that I had it in my hands.

I didn't think about how that love could actually ruin everything; how that kiss would change our lives for the worse.

I didn't think about how it would affect everyone. I wanted to be selfish for one second; I wanted to be happy.

I forgot to realize that sometimes, the most beautiful things are capable of destroying everything; that beauty is dangerous—and it's the most dangerous thing of all.

Chapter 34
The Sleepover

(7 years ago)

"You know, sometimes I wonder why Lucy here never gets a boyfriend." Bree said as she was sitting down on one of the couches in Libby's house. It was one of the biggest houses in town, so they almost always hold their sleepovers there. Libby's feet were propped on the table in front of her, and she was drinking some chardonnay. "I think no one wants her." She mocked. "Poor little sweet Lucy, always such a loser."

"What is wrong with you, Bree?" Lucy asked, drinking some more of the spiked tea from earlier. "Why do you always have to hate on me like that? I never did anything wrong to you. And in case you've forgotten, my parents gave you a home."

"You don't have to remind me." Bree said. "You're still a loser."

"A flirt and a loser." Libby said. "I mean, she was obviously flirting with Harper earlier. Right, Laurel?"

"All you girls are drunk." Laurel replied and drank some water. "Harper loves me, I'm not jealous."

"Touché." Bree raised an eyebrow and drank some more chardonnay. "And what about little Miss Angeline here? Don was flirting with you earlier, Anj! What's up with that?"

"He was not flirting with me." Angeline said. "You're obviously drunk, Bree."

"Right," Libby said. "And besides, why would Don flirt with Angeline? She's way out of my league."

"Of course I am," Angeline said. "I'm not like the rest of you."

This made them all surprised because Angeline barely talked that way. She was always nice and quiet and patient—what in the world happened?

"What did you say?" Bree asked.

"You are a bitch, Bree." Angeline said. "I won't be surprised if Tyler's going to leave you for someone else."

"What did you just say?!"

"Hey—" Libby tried to stop them. "Hey—"

But just then, Tyler called and broke up with Bree on the phone. She couldn't believe what she just heard. She couldn't believe that Tyler would break up with her like that.

"I'm sorry," he said, "I couldn't do this anymore."

"Couldn't do what?"

"This. Us." He replied. "I don't want to lie to you anymore, Bree. I don't want to hurt you anymore. I'm in love with someone else—"

"Don't say things like that. You're just drunk."

"No, I'm not. I'm the most sensible I've been in a while. I'm sorry. It's over."

So, she found herself in tears, not really wanting to talk to anyone. But she knew she wouldn't be able to keep it for long.

"What happened?" Lucy asked.

Bree looked at all of them. "It's over." She said. "He broke up with me." And she allowed herself to be consumed by her tears.

"What? But why?" Laurel asked.

"He said he was in love with someone else." Bree cried. "He said that he doesn't love me anymore. He's—" She then looked at Lucy. "This is your fault!" She said. "This is all your fault!"

"What does this have to do with me?"

"You were always in love with him. You tried to steal him from me. Oh I'm going to end you!" She said, went over to Lucy, and tried to strangle her.

"Bree, stop!" Laurel said. "You're drunk. You need to take a rest."

"We all need to take a rest." Libby said. "It's been a tough day. Come on. We can talk about this tomorrow." Because then, tomorrow was a reality, not just a possibility.

***

"Oh I'm gonna kill her!" Bree told Angeline and Laurel while they were in one of the guest bedrooms in Libby's house that evening. "She'll pay for this. I know she has something to do with this."

"Bree, calm down." Angeline said. "She's our cousin. And besides…you're not even sure that it's her whom Tyler is in love with. Everything is just a possibility; we're not sure what the truth is yet. Calm down."

"Angeline's right," Laurel said. "Just calm down. Everything is going to be okay."

"Oh, I hate you all!"

***

"She must've been really mad. I mean, I'd be, too, if Don breaks up with me by phone. But I'll ruin him, you know?" Libby laughed as she fixed the bed that she and Lucy will be sharing. "But I got to admit…I'm confused. Why would she think that you have something to do with their break up?"

Lucy took a deep breath. She didn't want to trust Libby about her feelings for Tyler, but she was also confused. Did Bree actually see them kiss? She then spoke. "You know how Bree hates me," Lucy said, "If I end up dead tomorrow, you already know who to blame."

We can all be biased sometimes.

Even the nicest, kindest person could have her own prejudices.

Just because someone's nice doesn't mean that she thinks that the world is fair and all that shit. Because at some point, we're all damaged-we're all flawed and we're all capable of thinking nasty things about the people around us.

The only problem is that more often than not, we think wrong of the people who we shouldn't think wrong about. Because our minds are twisted that way.

Our minds are programmed to believe the best in people we shouldn't trust, and be cynical about those we have to trust.

But who am I kidding?

No one is trustworthy; at least not in my group of so-called friends.

Chapter 35
The Killer

(7 years ago)

Lucy woke up in the middle of the night. She felt so hot, she needed to wash her face. It was the alcohol, she thought. She told herself that she probably should never drink again.

She opened the door to the bathroom. She was still half-asleep. She turned on the faucet and thought that it was going to be just another normal night of washing her face. Little did she know that it was the last time she would be able to do it.

The killer was already there, watching her; watching her every step—from the time she got out of the room to the time she went inside the bathroom. The killer was ready to put her plans to life—and end Lucy's life in the process.

The killer hated her before; hated her when she realized that there was something more to her than just being Tyler's friend; that she and Tyler had a past. She hated her even more when she saw her and Tyler kiss earlier.

That was the last straw, she decided.

She had long been in love with Tyler—way before Tyler and Bree got together, way before he talked to her days before prom, way before Bree and Tyler made up again.

This was the last straw.

After all, no one would suspect her of doing this. Among all of them, she was the cleanest. She was the smartest. She was the most caring—mother hen, that's what they usually called her.

The killer was Laurel.

She even laughed at this thought. Who would even think that poor, sweet, intelligent Laurel could kill someone?

Ha! Looks can really be deceiving.

Laurel went inside the bathroom and pulled Lucy's hair.

"Wh-what are you—" Lucy wasn't able to finish what she was saying. There was a lot of water in the faucet, flowing, going through different directions. Laurel pushed Lucy's head down the lavatory; pushed her so hard her face bruised; pushed her so hard she threw up.

She kept on throwing up; puke all over the floor, her head so dizzy she no longer knew what would come next.

Laurel tossed her to the toilet, pushed her head so hard that she would no longer be able to breathe; pushed her head so hard that she'd die surrounded by her own puke.

"I'm sorry, Lucy," She said, "But you deserved that. You deserved all of that." She slowly made her way out of the bathroom, went down to go to the first floor bathroom, and flushed the gloves that she was wearing. There would be no more evidence; everyone would think that it was all just an accident.

And if all else fails, they could all blame Bree.

She was the nastiest of them all. She was the bitch—but not Laurel; never Laurel.

She went back to bed with a wicked grin on her face.

***

"AHHHHHHH! HELP! WHERE ARE ALL OF YOU?! HELP!" Bree's screams sliced the silence of the morning, prompting everyone to wake up. Bree was shaking and so was Libby.

Lucy was lying on the floor, her face and hair wet, puke near the toilet and on the faucet. Lucy didn't look like a normal person anymore: her lips were dry, her hands were cold—everything about her was cold and lifeless. In short, she was no longer alive.

"Oh my god," Libby said, with tears in her eyes. "Oh my god, she's not breathing—she's---oh god no—"

"What's going on?" Laurel asked.

"I don't know." Bree answered, her hands shaking, "I was…I wanted to wash my face and pee and when I opened the door, I saw her with her head on the toilet and I…I didn't know what to do," She was crying so hard now that it scared the girls, "I wanted to get her attention and when I touched her, she fell and…oh god what are we gonna do? We'll be in a lot of trouble." She cried some more, which prompted Angeline to hug her.

They were all crying and in a state of panic now.

"We should call the police, right?" Angeline asked. "Or 911 or—"

"Don't you get it?" Libby asked, "We'll be in trouble. I'll be in trouble! You think my parents would—oh god—this is insane. Who would do this?!"

"It's probably an accident." Laurel said, "I mean…you guys were all drunk last night and maybe she had a little too much."

"And she ended up dead." Bree stated. "She shouldn't be dead. I mean…this is just…"

"Are you sure you didn't wake up last night?" Libby asked Bree. "You're fond of taunting her. I mean, maybe you were too drunk and you decided to—"

"What? Kill her?!" Bree said, "Are you insane?!"

"I didn't say that." Libby said. "But, it's just that things between you ended up on a bad note last night and I thought that maybe—"

"Oh don't be insane, Libby." Bree argued, "You're the one who slept in the same room with her! Maybe, this is your fault. Maybe, you put something on her drink or led her to the bathroom and—"

"You're ridiculous! Why would I even think of doing that? I have no anger whatsoever at Lucy, unlike you!"

"Guys, enough—"Angeline said, "No one wanted this to happen."

"How sure are you of that?" Libby asked.

"Guys—" Laurel said, "We can't just leave her here or...let's just call—"

"Libby?"

They were startled when they heard the voice of Libby's mother, Mrs. Amelia Kutcher.

"Oh god, oh god...we're all in trouble—" Libby stammered.

"Libby?" She called out again. "I came back early, your dad's taken a side trip to San Diego. Why the hell is this house trashed? Where are you?" She was then making her way up the stairs and the girls really didn't know what to do. They were just stuck in the bathroom, clinging to the last few moments of their sanity.

"Libby? Why aren't you speaking?" Amelia said as she arrived in the bathroom and opened the door wide. "What's going on—" She stopped when she saw Lucy dead on the floor. "Oh my god!" She called out. "What did you do?!"

"Mom," Libby cried, "It's—it's an accident."

"Oh it better be." Amelia said. "I'll call 911."

***

They were never able to talk to Libby again after that morning. Her parents didn't even let her attend Lucy's wake, or her funeral. Tyler didn't want to talk to them for a while. He also didn't attend the funeral.

The police said that it was an accident—like they always do when they have no idea how to solve a case; like they always do when they're too lazy to do their job.

"Do the two of you still think that I did this?" Bree asked Angeline and Laurel the day of Lucy's funeral. They were standing on one side of the cemetery, watching Lucy's body being buried to the ground.
"Let's not talk about this anymore." Laurel said, the perfect portrait of a griev-

ing girl in her black dress and veiled hat. "What happened already happened. Let's just let her rest in peace."

"Oh god, you actually do?" Bree asked with tears in her eyes. "You think I could kill someone?" She then looked at Angeline. "Anj? Even you?"

"Bree, let's just—"

"I can't believe you." Bree said. "I can't believe you both." She then ran away, ran far away from everyone, making everyone think that she was guilty; that she had something to be scared about.

Because she ran—and running is a sign of guilt.

But Laurel? No one would think that she's guilty. No one would think that she had something to do with this. No one would think that someone as pure and intelligent as she was could have something to do with her friend's death.

Laurel was safe.

Laurel was happy.

Laurel got everything she ever wanted.

Finding out the truth could shatter you more than you ever thought it would. Finding out the truth could make you realize that life really is so much more than it is; that you never really know who your true friends are.

That maybe, you've always been alone—and that will no longer change.

Finding out the truth could make you whole. It could make you understand everything that went on in the past, it could allow you to finally have peace. But at the same time, it could also break you.

It could break you because no matter what you think you know, the truth is so much different, so much bigger, than what it pretends to be.

And when that happens, you'd just have no idea about what to feel anymore.

To be honest, I have no idea if this was what I had always wanted in the first place.

To be honest, I have no idea what I want anymore.

I just don't know anymore.

All I want is to hurt Laurel—hurt her, hurt her so bad she wouldn't be able to get out of the house anymore.

I want to end her like she ended me.

I want justice.

I want revenge.

Chapter 36
She's Gone

Lucy left Cassiopeia's body and the circle broke. All of them were in tears; all of them heaving. With the help of Lucy, in Cassiopeia's body, and Tyler looking in Cassiopeia's eyes, they were all able to see what happened seven years ago. They were finally able to find out the truth about what happened to Lucy; about who betrayed who, and about who really was to blame.

"Oh god, I think I'm going to throw up." Libby said as she stood up and went near one of the curtained windows. She dropped to her knees and cried on the floor as Emmy tried to comfort her.

"I'm sorry." Emmy said.

Libby hiccupped, "All this time, I thought Bree was to blame…all this time I thought she had something to do with this because of how she hated Lucy back then. I didn't know that there was more to this."

"There's always more to everything." Audrina said.

"I can't believe Laurel did this." Libby cried. "I---I don't understand. I just don't understand. They thought I also had something to do with this because of the fact that I left Sky Valley but…Laurel?" There was a lot of fear in her eyes. "I don't know what to believe in anymore."

"It's all my fault." Tyler said, his voice full of pain. He was obviously scarred by what he just saw. He didn't want to look back on those times anymore and now that he did, he couldn't help but be consumed by guilt. "If…only I didn't get together with Bree and…if I didn't break up with her that way---"

"Laurel said that she always had feelings for you. Did you know that, Tyler?" Libby asked. "Did you know that?!" She asked through gritted teeth.

"She—she told me about it once." He said, his voice quivering. "When… when Bree and I broke up right before Senior Prom…but…but I didn't really believe her because you know, she's Laurel. She's different from us. I just…I told her maybe we could go together but then Bree said sorry, we made up, and I told Laurel I was sorry but I couldn't go with her—"

"And then you kissed Lucy."

"It was Lucy all along." He said. "I've always been in love with her but I didn't know how to tell her and all that. I wasn't—I wasn't thinking…"

"Oh you were such an ass!" Libby said. "Still are!"

"Libby—"

"Enough." Emmy told them. "Fighting won't do you guys any good. We already know the truth. We should just figure it out from here. We should…We should see Laurel—"

"And the cops—" Libby added.

"No, we have to do this by ourselves first." Audrina said.

"Where's Lucy, by the way?" Emmy asked. "Cassiopeia?"

"She's—she's not here." Cassiopeia said.

"What? Where is she?"

"She went over to Laurel's." Cassiopeia said. "She's raging mad. She's-"

"Oh god." Libby said.

"Come on." Emmy said and they used her car to drive to Laurel's house. It was a frustrating drive because of all the days there could be a parade in Sky Valley, this day is one of them. Some school kids were marching on the grounds followed by some women wearing various flowers on their body dancing and singing.

"Oh fuck off." Libby muttered.

"Calm down." Emmy said, but she was also getting a whole lot agitated already.

Finally, the marchers went on their way and they were able to speed through the ground to make their way to Laurel's house. Libby got out of the car first and knocked so hard on Laurel's door, Emmy was scared that all the neighbors will think they're making a commotion.

"Come out!" Libby shouted. "Come out, you dumbass!"

"Libby—"

"Come out, Laurel! You fucking liar!"

"Uhm, excuse me? Are you looking for Laurel Blake?" A woman, presumably in her early 30's said. She was wearing a straw hat and had a basket of fruits in her hand.

"Yes." Emmy answered. "Is she inside?"

"Oh, I'm sorry," the woman said, "She's no longer there."

"What do you mean?" Emmy asked, fearing what she already knows.

The woman looked at each of them and replied, "She's gone."

Into The Unknown

Chapter 37
Where Is She?

"She's gone," Laurel's neighbor said when they asked her where she was. Just those two words were almost enough to crush everyone's hopes. They wanted to talk to Laurel so they could bring her to the police and this could all finally end. But, apparently, she was no longer at home—and they had no idea where she was.

"I hate that bitch!" Libby said through gritted teeth. "She thinks she can get away with everything! How much of a bitch could she actually be—"

"Libby, enough," Emmy said.

"Is she okay?" the neighbor asked. "Is something wrong?"

"Uhm, no, I mean, yeah---I—," Emmy said and took a deep breath. "Do you happen to have any idea where Laurel is? I mean, we have to talk to her. It's extremely important."

"Oh, no," the neighbor said, "she doesn't really talk to us, you know? Always keeps to herself. But…I've heard she has family in Tallulah Falls. Her mother, Eleanor, lives there, if I'm not mistaken. I'm not sure where, but if it's really an emergency, then I'm sure you could find her there. Tallulah Falls is not a very big place, after all."

"Tallulah Falls," Audrina repeated. "That's not too far away. If we go now—"

"Yeah," Emmy said, and then turned to the neighbor again, "Thank you," she said. "We'll get going now."

"Alright then, you guys take care. It might rain in a while," She said, pertaining to the dark clouds above. "See you." She then went back to her own house and left Emmy and her group by themselves.

Lucy then turned up on the front porch. "Maybe we should all give up now," She said, tears in her eyes, sadness enveloping her voice. "I didn't really want this to happen. I mean—it's just…"

"Are you insane, Lucy?" Emmy asked. All of them turned to look at her. "We've come all the way for this. We've actually managed to find out who did this to you and now you want to give up? Sure, it's not easy. We have to go all the way to Tallulah Falls and we have to figure this all out again, but if we give up now then what would all of this mean? We're here, Lucy. We're doing all we can for you. So please, just trust us. Trust me. We'll find Laurel, we'll get her back here, and everything will finally be okay," She said with a conviction that even she started to believe in herself, no matter how scared and unsure she was.

"Should we go now?" Audrina asked.

"Yeah, but let me call someone first."

"Who?"

"Sara, from the police station. She's really nice and she's not like the rest of them," Emmy took her phone from her purse, dialed Sara's number, and spoke. "Yes, if you could just please track my number…yeah, go ahead and follow us. We're going to Tallulah Falls, yes. Please just trust me with this, Sara. Okay. Don't do anything until I say so, okay? Okay? Right. See you." She ended the call, put the phone back in her purse and turned to look at Audrina, Libby, Lucy, Cassiopeia, and Tyler, who were looking at her like their life depended on her.

"Let's go." She said and they piled into her car.

They were going to Tallulah Falls.

You're getting there.

You're finally going to learn everything you've always wanted to know, and yet, you're so scared. You're so scared because you have seriously no idea how this will go. You have no idea how to make sense of everything, how to feel like everything is going to be okay.

You're so scared because you know the closer you are to the truth and the more these crazy things happen, the worse you feel about the whole situation because it could drain you of all the energy you thought you had, because you'd only feel like the whole point of everything will be gone, because you'd have no idea about how to go from there.

But, you're still going to get there because if you don't then things would just be worse.

If you don't, there would be no sense to everything you've done in the past.

And that's definitely not what you want.

Chapter 38
Off To Tallulah Falls

Audrina thought that the drive from Sky Valley to Tallulah Falls was one of the weirdest she's ever had. No one was speaking, and she could no longer stomach the creepy, old roads leading to Tallulah. There were so many trees and she could see a bridge a couple of meters away from them. The Tallulah Falls Lake was visible already and somehow, the strong current of the water made her feel scared.

"Erm…so…Tyler, such hot stuff, aren't you?" She asked, breaking the silence. "You drove all these women to fight for you."

"Not me," Libby said. "I always thought you were trouble, Ty," she quipped and raised an eyebrow.

"Really? His charm didn't work for you?" Audrina asked.

Libby scoffed. "Duh," she said, "I always knew he was trouble. Just imagine, he was together with almost all of them. Two ended up dead, one's in prison, and one's…we still have no idea where. Nah-uh."

"This isn't my fault," Tyler said. "Or maybe it was. I don't know anymore."

"Well, let me break it down for you, sweetheart," Audrina said, "I don't think you've actually told us everything we need to know. And you know what? That sucks because we're all here trying to help you out and you repay us with this silence? What the hell is that about?"

"That's true," Cassiopeia said. "There are even parts of you that I can't read, like, you're trying to hide something from us."

"Is that true, Tyler?" Emmy asked, her eyes focused on the road. "What else do we need to know?"

Tyler took a deep breath. "It's not that easy, you know?" he said. "This isn't

171

easy for me."

"It's not easy for any of us, damn it," Libby said in frustration. "You think I actually wanted to go back to Sky Valley and have to go through everything again? No," she said. "I was living my own perfect life in Mountain Valley when these people came up to my door and told me I had to help my friend out. And you know what? As much as I didn't want to do it, I knew I had to because I knew that I at least owe Lucy the truth. And you do, too, Ty. You do."

Tyler looked at Libby and a look of understanding passed between them. Then, a few seconds later, Tyler took a deep breath and spoke. "Okay," he said, "I'll tell you everything. I'll tell you everything now."

Emmy stopped the car as they arrived at the opening of Caledonia Cascade, a bushy, tree-lined passage in Tallulah Falls. "Go on," she said and looked at Tyler. "Tell us what we need to know."

There are reasons why you cannot—and should not—be nostalgic all the time. For the most part, nostalgia is about looking back at the past. It's all about remembering who you were—who you used to be, what you used to do, what you used to eat, how you used to smell, how everything was one way at some point, and how everything seems to be different now.

Sometimes, it's good to look back.

It's good to remember how things have been because maybe, doing so would help you figure out how you came to be the way you are, and why everything changed.

Maybe it would give light to the situation. Then, after you look back, you can finally tell yourself to move on, and, if possible, forget about the things that hurt.

Nostalgia, just like everything in the world, has a positive and negative side to it.

And that's okay, you tell yourself.

That's okay.

Chapter 39
When We Were Young

(12 years ago)

Twelve-year-old Tyler Rowland was walking through the hallways of Sky Valley Middle School, trying to be invisible. Ever since he was young, people always wanted to spend time with him, get his attention, get in his clique; but today was one of those days when he wanted to be alone.

His parents just separated and he really didn't know how to react to it.

It was club organization day, he realized, as he saw the banner above him. Basically, it was a day when he and his schoolmates could join one of those clubs that they always wanted to join. He knew that most of his friends were joining the Sports Club. He was near the Math Club room, but who was he kidding? He wasn't a math genius.

Then, he saw one room at the end of the hallway with a card in front that said it was the Science Club. He had to admit, he loved science. He loved the process of discovering things, studying those things, and finding out how everything came to be.

Why not? He thought. Why not?

He went inside that room, knowing that he'd be joining Science Club, but not knowing that his life would change in a way he didn't expect.

***

Lucy always knew how it felt to be invisible. Her parents barely recognized her, and whenever they did, it was only to remind her that she had to ace her exams; that she had to be this and that. They never really told her they loved her. They never really made her feel how it was to have a parent.

Sure, they were there in a sense that they sent her to the best school, they bought her all she could ask for, but still…that wasn't enough because they were never there to make her feel like she actually had someone to count on. They were never there to make her feel like she was the number one person in their lives.

Today was a good day, though.

It was club organization day and Lucy was going to join the Science Club, the only club she has joined since she was a little girl. Science Club made her feel like somehow, she belonged—even for a few minutes or so. She loved how they dissected frogs, tried to make salted eggs, and used the craziest apparatus.

She opened the door to the Science Club room when, alas! Someone bumped into her, looking lost and confused. It was Tyler Rowland, resident cutie. Ever since they were classmates in kindergarten, he captured the attention of many. Some people even say that he's the generation's future prince charming—whatever that means.

Anyway, she was surprised to find him in this room because, well…what in the world would he be doing there? This isn't his world—he's not part of Lucy's world.

"Tyler Rowland?"

"Yeah, hi."

"What are you doing here?" Lucy asked, finally feeling authoritative, despite the fact that her hair was in braids and she had with her the biggest, pinkest backpack you'd ever see.

"Uhm…this is Science Club, right?" He said, all charming and cute and sweet. Why was it so hard not to notice him? It's like he could command everyone—even at an early age.

"Yeah. So…what are you doing here?" she asked.

"It's club organization day. I love science, so, why not?" Tyler responded.

"Really now…," Lucy said, "I never pegged you as a Science Club guy."

"There are still a lot of things you don't know about me, Lucy."

"Oh," Lucy muttered. "You love science, you say? So, who coined the Theory of Relativity, then?"

"That's easy," he answered with a smile on his face. "Albert Einstein, of course."

Lucy raised an eyebrow. "Well…," she said, "What can you say about the migration of the Queen Alexandria Birdwing—"

"Uhm, that species doesn't usually migrate," he answered confidently. "Monarchs do, though."

Despite herself, Lucy found herself smiling. "Okay, then, maybe you're really a science guy."

He laughed. "Passed your test, didn't I?"

"Welcome to the club."

And since that moment, Lucy and Tyler were friends. Everything was going so well that she even invited him to her 12th birthday party—a big, Hawaiian-inspired one complete with sliders, some inflatable pools, slip n' slides, and kebabs. It was a luau through and through.

Lucy felt great. For the first time in a long while, she felt like her parents could finally see her; that they finally loved her. For the first time in a long time, she felt like they were there for her. Maybe it was only because she was turning 12 today and it was a big deal, but she'd take whatever she could get.

"Hey, beautiful," Tyler said as he came up to her while she was sitting on a bench in their backyard, wearing her tankini, floral shorts, and a lei on her neck, of course.

"Hey." She smiled at him. She was happy that he arrived. She had been waiting for him, but she knew he had been cornered by some of his friends and she didn't want to cause a commotion. All she wanted was to spend time with him.

"I left your gift in the living room," he said.

"Oh, you really didn't have to bring anything," Lucy said, surprised.

"No, I wanted to," he said, "and…well, there's something else."

"What do you mean?"

"Luce…I…well…I really like you, you know? Like—"

"Like?" She couldn't believe what she just heard. Did Tyler just admit that he liked her liked her?

"Like…," he muttered, at a loss for words, "like this." He moved closer to Lucy and kissed her softly on the lips. The kiss lasted only for a second or so but it already meant a lot to Lucy. At that moment, she felt it was the best thing that had ever happened to her. It was definitely the best birthday gift ever.

"Ty—"

He smiled at her and she smiled back.

"You know—" he said, but he was interrupted by Lucy's parents who came to the backyard with her cousins Bree and Angeline in tow. Their mother, Margaret, was with them, too. She knew that her cousins would be coming today but she didn't want them to come right at the moment when she had her first kiss.

"Hi!" Bree greeted them and went up to Lucy. "Happy Birthday." She smiled. "Thanks, Bree," Lucy said. She noticed how shiny and beautiful Bree's hair was; how she seemed to be confident being in their house, being who she was. She didn't have a semblance of shyness on her. She was definitely the opposite of Lucy.

"Luce, you better help Bree and Angeline get their stuff ready," Lucy's mother smiled. "We're sorry we didn't tell you earlier but…they're going to stay with us now."

"You mean for the summer?"

"No," Lucy's father said. "They'll be staying with us for good. Margaret and Tommy broke up and she has no one else but us—"

Her father's words were drowned by the noise around her, and inside her head. She didn't want to listen to him. She didn't want to share her parents with anyone else but then again, they were never really hers in the first place.

This party may not even have been for her.

This party was meant as a housewarming gift for her cousins.

Her parents don't love her—they never really did.
***
Later that evening, Lucy opened Tyler's gift in her room. She was happy to see that it was a cuddly stuffed gray Grizzly bear. She hugged it right away and smiled at it and was about to call Tyler on the phone when suddenly, her cousin Bree entered the room.

"Hi," Bree greeted. There was something rotten about her, Lucy thought, something wicked; something she really couldn't point out.

"Hey," Lucy shot back.

Even at 12, Bree already looked like a real teenager: she was slim, her hair beautiful, and she was so full of poise; she could already pass for a model.

"What is that?" Bree asked. "Did that boy earlier gave that to you?"

"What? Uhm…yeah, that's Tyler's gift."

"Tyler," Bree repeated. "That's a nice name." She smiled and took the bear from Lucy. "You guys together?"

"No—no."

"Oh, good," Bree quipped. "Because I like him."

"What did you say?"

"Don't play dumb with me, Luce," Bree said. "You heard me. I said I like him. He's cute. And, besides, your parents told us you weren't allowed to have a boyfriend yet so…dibs on him, I say."

"Bree, this is none of your business. And give me that bear back."

"Oh, no, honey, this is mine now," Bree said. "You're not going to take this bear back from someone who never had something like this before, would you?"

Lucy took a deep breath. She wanted to do something but she really didn't know how to react to this.

"Thought so," Bree said. "Let's just be clear, Luce," she went on, "what's yours is mine now. We're going to live here. And we both know that your father is fonder of us than of you, so…if you want us all to live in peace then be good." She put a smile back on her face. "Thanks."

She then made her way out of the room. "Goodnight, Luce," She said before closing the door behind her.

There are some people who get what they want because they know they can get it right away.

I don't know if it's wrong that they do not work hard for it; I don't know if it's wrong that they don't work doubly hard for what they want, but then again… life is unfair. It really is unfair. So, you take what you can, and give what you can, and that's that.

But looking back, I wished that I stood up to Bree right at that moment. I wished that I told her how I really felt and that I didn't give up on Tyler right away.

Because even if you feel like you're competing with the most beautiful person in the world, when you know that you have it in you to survive, and that you're the type of person who's willing to fight for what she wants, and what she deserves, then you should do it.

If I did, maybe none of this would have happened.

Maybe, we'd all be living happily ever after.

Chapter 40
We Used To Be Friends

"Luce? Luce, wait!" Tyler called out as he saw Lucy walking towards the library one afternoon. It was a couple of days after he kissed her on her 12th birthday party and he was shocked at how things turned out. She stopped speaking to him after that evening, and now she was acting like they weren't friends. In fact, it already made him feel like an idiot because people were snickering as he tried to get her attention. He, Tyler Rowland, was seeking the attention of one of the most unpopular girls in school.

"Lucy!" He said as he finally caught up with her.

She looked at him and took a deep breath. He thought that her eyes were swelling, like she had been crying a lot.

"Lucy, what's going on? Is there any problem? You haven't spoken to me since—"

"Let's not talk about it," she said. "There's nothing to talk about."

"What?" he asked, confused. He always thought that somehow, they understood each other; that even though they haven't really recognized it, they were actually in love with each other, that they had feelings for each other, even at an early age. "I thought—" His voice was full of hurt and even Lucy felt it.

"Well, you thought wrong," she said.

"Lucy, I don't understand."

"There's nothing to understand," she muttered and before the tears could come rushing out of her eyes and before she could say another word, she ran away from him, determined not to look back.

"Damn it," Tyler said as he watched Lucy run away from him.

"What's wrong? Did my cousin do anything?" Just then, Bree, Angeline, Lib by, and Laurel came together with their friends Don and Harper.

"Yeah, man, what happened?" Don asked. For a 12 year old, he was already big and bulky—and knew that someday, he could take over this town, too.

"Nothing," Tyler said, "Nothing at all."

"You could have lunch with us," Laurel smiled kindly.

"Yeah, we can sit together," Bree smiled, too.

And ever since that day, Tyler started to hang out with them. Sometimes, Lucy would be around but she would never talk to Tyler. He didn't really know how to feel about that because he knew that he didn't do anything wrong, and he didn't want her to get hurt in any way. He wanted to talk to her, up to the point that he was spending a lot of time with Bree, but still, Lucy wouldn't budge.

And then one day, shortly before Junior Prom, he and Bree got together. All he remembered about that day was that they were in one of those parties that Lucy's parents organized when suddenly, Lucy's parents asked Bree if she was dating anyone, and she said she was dating Tyler, and soon, everyone thought that they really were a couple and Tyler didn't know how to deny it anymore. He actually didn't know why he aided her in her lie, but then again, he was growing up without a girl in sight. Lucy wasn't talking to him, and nothing felt right.

He saw how Lucy escaped from that party, though. He wanted to follow her, talk to her, make things right, but he could no longer get rid of Bree.

From then on, he knew that the life he was living was already a lie—and he chose to do nothing about it. For him, at that point, it was better to have a lie of a life than nothing at all.

Lies.

Here's the thing: everyone lies. And I mean everyone.

Tell me about someone who hasn't lied anytime in his life, white lies included. I'm pretty sure you wouldn't be able to.

That's because it's human nature to lie.

Lies are around because some people say that they have to tell lies to protect the people they love. People lie because they want to hide something that could hurt the people they love; they want to pretend that everything is okay, and that there are no big problems whatsoever.

But if you'd ask me, I'd say that people lie not because they want to protect the people around them, but mostly because they want to protect themselves.

Because if they don't, they'd end up hurt. If they don't, the truth will come out and they wouldn't have any idea how to deal with it.

Lies are hurtful; deceiving. Lies shouldn't be around.

But they are.

They are—and they always will be.

Chapter 41
Why Are You Such A Bitch?

(7 years ago)

It was a couple of days before Senior Prom and Tyler and Bree had been together for over a year now. Today was one of those days when they were fighting again.

Tyler was getting tired of it all; all they ever did was fight. They fought about the simplest things, like if Bree's outfit was good enough for the day, or about the time when Tyler was going to pick her up from home. He hated picking her up from home because usually, Lucy was there, and there was this inevitable air of sadness around them; an air that was also full of pain and guilt. It was all getting confusing and Tyler was trying to find a way to break things off with Bree but he didn't know how.

"What are you thinking about?" Bree asked as they were walking to school that day.

"Nothing," he said, fixing the way he carried his bag.

"Hey, look at me," she said and made him face her. "That's not the face of someone who has nothing in mind. What's going on?"

"Nothing."

At that moment, Lucy passed them by. She was wearing a Robin's Egg Blue dress and didn't really mind Bree and Tyler until Bree called her out. "What are you wearing, Kimmy?! That's super 90's. Or no, make that super 50's. It's a small town but you can grow up!"

Lucy looked at Bree and came up to them. She was obviously not in a good mood. "What is your problem?" she asked.

"Wow. Standing up to me now, huh?" Bree quipped. "This is new. Have you been taking anything?"

"Enough, Bree," Lucy seethed. "You're living in my house."

"In your parents' house."

"You go back to California if you have a problem with me. You have everything you want, what else do you need?"

"Hey—" Tyler tried to stop them.

"What did you just say?" Bree said.

"Bree? Luce?" Angeline said from behind them. "What's going on? You guys going to school?"

"I was just about to," Lucy said. She then looked at Angeline and smiled. "You want to come with?"

"Sure," Angeline smiled. "You two? Will you be okay?"

"Suck it, Anj," Bree muttered.

"Let's go," Lucy told Angeline and they continued walking, trying to keep their dresses from being fluttered by the wind.

Tyler took a deep breath and turned to Bree. "Why are you always such a bitch?" he asked. "Why can't you lay off her, even for once?"

"Wow, where is this coming from?"

"You know what, Bree? I'm getting fed up," he said. "You act like you're this super bitch whom everyone's supposed to love when clearly, there's nothing lovable about you. I'm staying with you because I'm trying to live with this lie that you created and you mess things up for everyone else! What the hell is wrong with you?!"

Bree laughed then stopped for a second, her eyes full of anger. "You know what?" she said. "Fine. You want to go after Little Miss Lucy? Do it. Let's see who comes running back to me."

"Fine," he said.

"Fine," she shot back, screamed for a bit, then left him alone on the sidewalk.

***

"Hey," Laurel greeted as she saw Tyler sitting by himself on the grass at the back on the school. It was a warm, windy day, and he didn't feel like having lunch at the cafeteria where everyone could see him. "I bought you a grilled cheese sandwich," she said, and before he could hesitate, she added, "And don't worry, it's on me." She smiled. "You shouldn't really sulk on an empty stomach, you know," she said as she sat down beside him, not minding if her yellow prairie dress got dirty.

"Thanks, Laurel," he said.

"I heard you guys fought."

"Yeah…." he said, "you know how much of a bitch she could be some days. I just wish she would stop, you know?"

"Well…old habits die hard," she said with a sly smile on her face. "It's a shame prom's coming up."

"Who are you going with?"

"Me? No one," Laurel said. "I'd probably just skip it altogether."

"Nah, don't do that," he said. "At this rate, she and I probably won't be going together. So…uhm…you know, if you don't mind, maybe we could—"

"Go to prom together?" She finished for him. "Oh my god, Bree would kill me."

"No, as friends of course."

"Yeah, yeah, of course," she said, with a hint of hurt in her voice. "Yeah, why not?"

"Alright." He smiled at her and she smiled back. "Thanks again…for everything."

"Don't mention it."

*** ***

It was two days before prom when Bree decided to talk to Tyler and air what she had in mind. "Look," she said, while they were standing by the door of the library, "I know you really wouldn't want to talk to me but…I care about you," she said. "And…and I wouldn't want this relationship to go to waste. I mean, it's not too late to start over, right? We can still be together. We can manage."

"Or you just want to have someone to go to prom with?"

"Don't be ridiculous. I love you, Ty. Ever since we were kids. So, please… just…give me a chance? Give us a chance? Let's not let what we have go to waste because of a petty fight."

He took a deep breath. How could he say no to Bree? She was asking for forgiveness. She told him that she loved him. And for what it's worth…she's been there for him all these years, cheering on him, being his guide. He wanted that girl to be Lucy, but somehow, Lucy didn't want to be that girl. Maybe, it was high time that he moved on—even if his heart was telling him otherwise.

"Alright," he said. "Okay."

"Okay?"

"Yeah," he answered. "I'm sorry, too. I didn't mean to call you a—"

"It's okay," she smiled. "Forget it. Come on, I think the cafeteria's selling something nice today."

"When did the cafeteria ever sell something nice?"

They looked at each other and cracked up.

*** ***

The night of prom was a night of fun, at least for most of the students. The auditorium was covered in sheets of pink and yellow, all cheery and bright, how most people deemed Sky Valley to be.

Bree went to the powder room so Tyler and Laurel were left alone at their table. Lucy was dancing somewhere with Libby and one of the boys.

"Hey," Tyler said to Laurel.

"Hey," she shot back and drank a Virgin Piña Colada.

"Look…about the uhm…when I asked you to—"

"You don't have to explain, Ty," she said. "I mean…she's your girlfriend and I'm just…nobody. We're all just nobodies to you."

"Laurel, that's not true."

"Yeah, well." She raised an eyebrow.

Bree then came back, her face full of happiness and excitement for the evening. "Serious talk?"

"No," Laurel said. "Let me go to the powder room." She left them alone.

"What was that about? Is she mad at me or anything?"

"No," Tyler said. "Let me go get us some drinks."

And once again, Tyler was placed in a web of confusion, mostly because of his own doing.

We have the power to confuse ourselves more than anything and anyone else in the world.

This is because we're supposed to know ourselves better than anyone else can.

But when we do not know ourselves, we pay the price of being rained on by confusion, and that's never a good thing.

When you're confused, your mind gets so cloudy that your judgment, more than anything, suffers from it. When you're confused, you don't get to be the kind of person you want to be. You don't often get what you want because you keep on choosing all these things that have nothing to do with your life.

Chapter 42
The Break-Up

It was a hot, sweltering afternoon and Lucy felt that her ruffled yellow taffeta dress was so hot and unflattering that it made her look like a cupcake. She didn't even know why she agreed to be in this tea party, except for the fact that her mother was one of the organizers and it would be such a shame if she wouldn't be there.

She was already so tired and she really didn't want to spend much time with Bree and all her friends because of their banter. She was tired of being with them, period.

Truth be told, there was only one person she wanted to spend time with, but it had been too long since they had time alone. It's not like she could still be with him because he had a girlfriend, and that girl was Bree, her cousin.

Lucy took a deep breath and tried to drown her sorrows in the tea that Libby spiked earlier. She drank as much as she could, trying to calm her stomach down because she wasn't a big drinker. Oh boy, she couldn't stomach the scent of chardonnay—it was just too much.

"You really shouldn't be drinking alone, you know?" Tyler said from behind her. He found her by the bushes and decided to sit down with her, never mind if their clothes got dirty. He also didn't want to be surrounded by everyone anymore and truth be told, he also didn't want to spend time with Bree. She could be too bitchy and she really wasn't his type.

Sometimes, he hated himself for ever trying to get Bree's attention and making her fall in love with him because he knew how wrong it was. It wasn't the best thing he had done in his life and he was ashamed of it. He actually wanted to be with Lucy but she stopped talking to him ages ago and he still didn't know why.

Lucy looked at Tyler, who had a hip flask in his hand. "What are you doing here?" she asked.

"I don't know," he said. "Maybe I want to be alone, too."

"Go somewhere else."

"Why are you so mad at me? What did I do to you?"

Lucy took a deep breath and drank some more tea. She noticed the roses swaying through the wind. "I don't think we should talk about that."

"No, really, why? Because as far as I'm concerned, I did nothing wrong to you. In fact, after that kiss on your 12th birthday, I wanted things to be better between us, to be a couple and all that but you just disappeared. Why?"

"It's none of your business."

"Really? Because I love you. You know that? I love you and all I've done these past couple of years is try to be close to you again, even having a relationship with Bree in the process. I know it's wrong but…oh whatever!" He then made Lucy face him and kissed her passionately on the lips. She pulled back at first but decided to let go of all her inhibitions; this was what she always wanted, anyway, and it was finally happening. The kisses were soft, beautiful…they were everything she had ever dreamed of and more.

"I love you, Luce."

"I love you, too," she said. "But this isn't right. I don't want Bree to get hurt."

"She'll be okay. I'll end things right now. I'll end things and sure, she'll get mad, but she'll move past it. Your cousin's tough. I don't want to hurt her anymore by pretending that I'm in love with her when I'm really not. I don't want this craziness to continue anymore. I want to make things right."

"But---but she'll hate me. She'll hate us."

"She won't hate you, Luce," he said. "No one saw us kiss. It will be okay."

"You'll really break up with her?"

"Yes," he said. "I'll do anything for you. I'll do anything for us."

"Oh, Tyler," she said and hugged him. They stayed like that for a little while, thinking that no one saw them and that they were safe. They thought they had the whole world in their hands and that they'd finally get whatever it is that they're hoping for, but the truth is far stranger than that.

***

"You know, sometimes I wonder why Lucy here never has a boyfriend," Bree said as she was sitting down on one of the couches in Libby's house. It was one of the biggest houses in town, so they almost always hold their sleepovers there. Libby's feet were propped on the table in front of her, and she was drinking some chardonnay. "I think no one wants her," she mocked. "Poor little sweet Lucy, always such a loser."

"What is wrong with you, Bree?" Lucy asked, drinking some more of the spiked tea from earlier. "Why do you always have to hate on me like that? I never did anything wrong to you. And in case you've forgotten, my parents gave you a home."

"You don't have to remind me," Bree said. "You're still a loser."

"A flirt and a loser," Libby said. "I mean, she was obviously flirting with Harper earlier. Right, Laurel?"

"All you girls are drunk," Laurel replied and drank some water. "Harper loves me, I'm not jealous."

"Touché," Bree raised an eyebrow and drank some more chardonnay. "And what about little Miss Angeline here? Don was flirting with you earlier, Anj! What's up with that?"

"He was not flirting with me," Angeline said. "You're obviously drunk, Bree."

"Right," Libby said. "And besides, why would Don flirt with Angeline? She's way out of our league."

"Of course I am," Angeline said. "I'm not like the rest of you."

This made them all surprised because Angeline barely talked that way. She was always nice and quiet and patient—what in the world happened?

"What did you say?" Bree asked.

"You are a bitch, Bree," Angeline said. "I won't be surprised if Tyler's going to leave you for someone else."

"What did you just say?!"

"Hey—" Libby tried to stop them. "Hey—"

But just then, Tyler called and broke up with Bree on the phone. She couldn't believe what she just heard. She couldn't believe that Tyler would break up with her like that.

"I'm sorry," he said, "I can't do this anymore."

"Can't do what?"

"This. Us," he replied. "I don't want to lie to you anymore, Bree. I don't want to hurt you anymore. I'm in love with someone else—"

"Don't say things like that. You're just drunk."

"No, I'm not. I'm the most sensible I've been in a while. I'm sorry. It's over."

She found herself in tears, not really wanting to talk to anyone. But she knew she wouldn't be able to keep it for long.

"What happened?" Lucy asked.

Bree looked at all of them. "It's over," she said. "He broke up with me." She allowed herself to be consumed by her tears.

"What? But, why?" Laurel asked.

"He said he was in love with someone else," Bree cried. "He said that he doesn't love me anymore. He's—" She looked at Lucy. "This is your fault!" she shouted. "This is all your fault!"

"What does this have to do with me?"

"You were always in love with him. You tried to steal him from me. Oh I'm going to end you!" she said, went over to Lucy, and tried to strangle her.

"Bree, stop!" Laurel said. "You're drunk. You need to take a rest."

"We all need to take a rest," Libby said. "It's been a tough day. Come on. We can talk about this tomorrow." At that time, tomorrow was a reality, not just a possibility. They had no idea that in just a couple of hours, their lives would change—and it wouldn't be for the better.

***

They were never able to talk to Libby again after that morning. Her parents didn't even let her attend Lucy's wake, or her funeral. Tyler didn't want to talk to them for a while. He also didn't attend the funeral.

The police said that it was an accident—like they always do when they have no idea how to solve a case; like they always do when they're too lazy to do their job.

"Do the two of you still think that I did this?" Bree asked Angeline and Laurel the day of Lucy's funeral. They were standing on one side of the cemetery, watching Lucy's body being buried to the ground.

"Let's not talk about this anymore," Laurel said, the perfect portrait of a grieving girl in her black dress and veiled hat. "What happened already happened. Let's just let her rest in peace."

"Oh god, you actually do?" Bree asked with tears in her eyes. "You think I could kill someone?" She then looked at Angeline. "Anj? Even you?"

"Bree, let's just—"

"I can't believe you," Bree said. "I can't believe you both." She ran away, ran far away from everyone, making everyone think that she was guilty; that she had something to be scared about.

***

Tyler stayed behind.

Tyler stayed when everyone else went home. He stayed so he could spend some time by Lucy's grave. He wanted to talk to her, show her how he really felt—even for the last time.

But, he couldn't find the right words to express how he felt.

He didn't know how to tell her how he really felt. He didn't know how to finally admit that he loved her, that she was on his mind, that he will never forget her. So, he stayed quiet.

He stayed quiet and stayed there, not knowing that Laurel was actually still there, too. For a while, they just stayed in front of Lucy's grave, not saying anything, not knowing how to make anything right.

There was an inn nearby. They were too young, but they had fake ID's. They were shattered, that's what he thought. They were both shattered by what happened. So, they spent the night together. They had sex, plain and simple.

When he brought her home that evening, he vowed to call her, but he never did.

He vowed to make things right, whatever that meant—but he never did.

So, he couldn't tell them this.

He drank himself into oblivion that evening. He drank his sorrows away, he didn't want to feel like today of all days, he found the courage to do something wrong; to do what he knew would hurt everyone around them.

He tried to forget.

He never spoke to Laurel about it again.

He never spoke to anyone about it, ever.

And today, he still wouldn't want to talk about it.

It's a secret that he would like to take to his own grave—and it would stay that way for always.

There are secrets we can never share with others. That's why they're considered "secrets", you know? These are the things that you would never want others to know; things that you'd rather keep to yourself.

More often than not, when you tell these secrets to others, you give them power to hurt you—to destroy you.

When you let these secrets come out in the open, it's like you're giving those secrets the chance to bring you down.

And there's nothing worse than to be brought down by your own secrets—because that means that you're the culprit—that you're the exact same person who brought yourself down.

And that's why some people vow to take their secrets with them to their graves—because then, they could both haunt each other, and the world could go on the way it usually does.

Chapter 43
The Photograph

(Present Day)

"So…that's it?" Libby asked Tyler as he told them the story of how he met Lucy and how at some point, he connected with Laurel. "You asked her to prom as a substitute, then you got back together with Bree, and then she decided to kill Lucy because you guys kissed at that tea party. Wow…really."

"Don't be ridiculous, Lib," he said. "You spiked their drinks, too. You have a fault in this, too."

"And now it's my fault?" Libby asked and laughed in a mocking manner. "Look, just because I spiked those drinks doesn't mean that I was the reason why everyone's heads were cracked that evening. Laurel did what she did because she was into you, and she wasn't able to confide in anyone about it before. And besides, Tyler, you're the one at fault. You played them all."

"Quit it, you two," Emmy said. "But, Ty…she's right. I feel like there's still something you're not telling us about."

"I told you everything I could tell."

"Could?" Libby asked. "See? So this means that you're really hiding something from us. Why don't you stop lying, Tyler?"

"I am not lying."

"Refusing us the truth is lying."

"I can see you're hiding something," Cassiopeia said.

"Read me, then."

"I can't." Cassiopeia replied. "You're not allowing me to."

"But if you're so good—"

"I said quit it," Emmy said. "You think all this bickering will help us? You think this will solve the case? You know what? I don't think it will. So, Tyler, if there's something you're hiding from us, you better tell us right now."

"I need to talk to Laurel first."

Emmy sighed. "Yeah, about that…" She then looked at Cassiopeia, "I don't know where she lives. Could you help us out?"

"Tyler," Cassiopeia said, "Do you have anything you own from the past… like, an old thing, from when you were still friends and all? That would help me track her down."

"Yeah, yeah, sure…," he said and pulled out his wallet.

"Oh my god, you're still using that?" Libby asked, as she saw the old leather wallet that Tyler used to own in high school. "He used to have that all the time! Are you like, stuck in the past or something?"

Tyler ignored her, opened the wallet, and took out an old photo of him, Don, Harper, Libby, Laurel, Angeline, Bree, and Lucy. It was taken on their prom night. They looked happy, but it was evident in their eyes that each of them was worried about something. "Here," he said, handing the photo to Cassiopeia.

Libby looked at it. "Oh man, you still have that," she said. "We were so young! I remember being so worried about finals then." She laughed. "If only I knew that death would come later, I wouldn't have been so worried."

"But of course, you didn't know," Cassiopeia said. "The human mind isn't always capable of thinking about the worst. We make ourselves believe that we can have what we want right away; that things will be easy. But of course, real life isn't always that way."

"You're weird," Libby quipped, "but awesome." She smiled. "Have you always had this…gift?"

"Ever since I was a little girl," Cassiopeia answered. "But enough about me." She smiled, placed a hand over the photo, and closed her eyes. She saw Laurel as a young girl, Laurel at the time of Lucy's death; Laurel at her grave, talking to someone, Laurel crying… There were so many tears, so many tears she had no idea someone could actually cry that much; a lot of evil energies; pain, shame, guilt… A house…a house three streets away, a peach colored house. It was a sad house with a sad person living inside. She will escape…they have to go now…they have to go now…

"What happened?" Audrina asked. "Did you see anything?"

"She's in a house three streets away," she answered. "We can leave the car here, it's a steep road up there. It's not too far, though, but we have to go now."

"I'll stay here," Audrina said. "I'll guide the police when they come."

"Okay," Emmy said. "Be careful."

"You guys should be careful," Audrina told them.

They were finally going to see Laurel, and Lucy could no longer speak, because she didn't really know how to feel about all of this.

She didn't know how to tell them that she was able to read Tyler's mind and see that he had sex with Laurel the day Lucy was buried.

And it wasn't the nicest feeling in the world.

Once again, she felt betrayed.

Betrayal is one of the worst things that can happen in life. But it gets even worse when you know that the person who once betrayed you is still betraying you because he thinks that you have no idea about what's happening.

It hurts.

You want to scratch him so badly that blood will ooze from every pore. You want to hurt him so badly that he will no longer realize who he is. You want to hurt him, decapitate him, make him remember why he should never have hurt you before.

But you can't.

You can't because despite everything, you still care.

Despite everything, you still need him.

And despite everything, you still love him.

Love could be your biggest traitor, you see, and that's something that will never change, even in death.

Chapter 44
That's Where She Lives

"If only we weren't trying to figure out what really went wrong in Laurel's head, I'd say that this walk seems nice," Libby quipped as they were walking by the tree-lined paths of Cascade Bridge in Tallulah Falls, the breeze from the waterfalls nearby giving the air some chill.

"Haven't been going out a lot in Mountain Valley?" Tyler asked.

"Yeah, well…" She took a deep breath. "My parents were scared that something would happen to me, or that I would dabble into something that I'm not meant to do. Believe me, I felt like a prisoner all the time. Even in college, they were still very strict. I wasn't allowed to live in a dorm, I wasn't allowed to go out on Friday nights and just have fun. I wanted to quit college altogether but then again, I wouldn't want to spend all day with my mother, you know?" She went on, "Then, in college, I fell in love. I know I broke Don's heart when I left but it was better for him-I guess his wife's amazing. At least, he got married, you know? I was supposed to be married but my mother wouldn't let me, so I finished school, and I told them they'd better let me live alone or I'd destroy them. Of course, I wouldn't have, but you know…"

Libby took a deep breath. "I guess you could say that even if I wasn't in Sky Valley, Lucy's death still affected me through and through. What about you, Ty? You seemed to have a carefree life, eh? You even dated Angeline."

"Don't add Angeline into all this. Let her rest in peace."

Libby sighed. "I don't even know what they saw in you."

"Fine, it's my fault, Are you happy now?"

"Guys, please!" Emmy said. "You keep fighting and you never solve anything. If you could just keep quiet then everything will be better, okay?"

"Sorry, ma'am," Libby quipped sarcastically.

"Where's Lucy, by the way? Isn't she speaking or anything?"

"She's here," Emmy answered. "She's just…a little too quiet."

"Yeah, and why is that?"

"She knows something," Cassiopeia said. "I can sense it."

"What?" Tyler asked, surprised. "I mean…what does she know?"

"Something important…she's trying to hold it in, though…" She stopped as they arrived in front of a lovely peach house flanked by peach trees and some sunflowers on the ground. "That's the house. Laurel's there."

They all looked at each other.

"Come on," Libby said. "Let's show the bitch how it's done."

Just because people can't see you doesn't mean that you won't feel hurt anymore. You can get used to anything, sure, but you have to admit that pain can still get through to you—no matter who or what you are.

Pain is toxic.

Pain is something that should be killed; something that no one should feel.

But then again, who am I kidding?

Without pain, things would be different.

Without pain, no one would feel the meaning of true joy.

Without pain, you may never be able to find out the truth, let it swallow you whole.

And I'm determined to put things to an end now, no matter what the cost.

I'm determined to be at peace, hopefully, when all of this is over.

Chapter 45
Mother Doesn't Know Best

"Libby," Emmy said, grabbing Libby by the arm. "You promise me that you will calm down, okay? Don't do anything you'll regret tomorrow. Don't do anything that will sabotage this."

"You don't have to ask me twice." Libby said and went up the staircase to knock on the door. Emmy, Tyler, and Cassiopeia were trailing behind. Lucy was floating near Emmy, her eyes focused only on the house.

Libby knocked on the door and put her hands in the pockets of her dress.

"That's a really nice dress," Emmy quipped.

"Thanks."

Then, someone opened the door. It was a woman presumably in her early 50's, with curly brown hair, and who had the look of someone regal; someone who's should be respected in the community. Libby would know her from anywhere because she spent countless times in her house in Sky Valley, and she was wearing her trademark pearl necklace.

The woman was none other than Laurel's mom, Leona.

There was a look of shock that crossed her face as her eyes traveled from Libby to Tyler. "Olivia." She muttered. "And...Tyler," she said as she played with the pearls on her neck. "What a surprise," she said, though it was obvious that she didn't mean it.

"Hi, Leona," Libby greeted and gave her a peck on the cheek. "How are you doing?"

"I'm...good," Leona replied, and it was obvious that she was nervous. "What brings you here? I thought you were already in Mountain Valley..."

"Yeah, I was," Libby said. "I still am, but you know...I thought that we could visit your daughter. I haven't seen her in ages and my god, I miss her! You know Tyler already, right? He just lost his fiancée recently, so-"

"I heard," Leona said. "Very unfortunate, isn't it?"

"Yeah," Tyler replied. "Very." His mind was somewhere else, too.

"Anyway," Libby continued, "I'd like you to meet our friends, Emmy and Cassiopeia. They're helping—"

"Us grieve," Tyler finished for her. "Libby and I stayed friends—"

"I didn't know about that," Leona said.

"Yeah, maybe there are some things Laurel's not telling you," Libby smiled slyly.

"You know, Libby, we'd love to have you around—and you guys, too," She looked at everyone, "but it's a very busy day for us right now and Laurel's—"

"Trying to escape through the back door?" Tyler said.

Everyone was surprised except for Leona. Tyler then forced his way inside and so did the others.

"Help! I'll call the police—Stop that—"

Tyler got to Laurel first and pinned her down on the ground. "Don't you dare try to escape from this! Don't you—"

"Oh, don't you dare call the police!" Libby took the phone from Leona and locked the door. "You stay right here or I'll hurt you."

"It's okay, Mom," Laurel said. "It's okay." She coughed. "It's okay."

She tried to stand up but Tyler was about to hold her again.

"Ty, stop," Emmy said, seeing that Laurel could be hurt.

"What do you want?" Laurel asked Tyler. "What did you come here for? And you, too, bitch?" She asked Libby.

"Asks the girl who killed her friend."

Laurel laughed. "You think you're so good now that you know that? What if I tell you that there's more to it than that?" She looked at Tyler. "What if I tell them about what happened the day we buried dear little Lucy?"

"This isn't the right time for that." Tyler said.

"What does that mean?" Libby was confused.

"We're here because you have to tell us what happened the day Lucy died. We're here because you owe us the truth. We all owe Lucy the truth."

When someone says that you have to be honest so someone can be set free, you need to understand where exactly that person is coming from.

Because how exactly could someone want to be honest when he knows that he himself is lying?

How could you trust someone who's already lied one too many times, who brought you to your destruction, who's possibly one of the reasons why you are where you are right now, even though he says that he didn't mean it?

Well, the answer is because sometimes people have to lie because it's the only thing they're used to. People have to lie because they think it could make things better. And you should trust them, maybe for the last time, so you can finally get the peace you deserve.

Chapter 46
You Never Really Loved Her

Laurel laughed. "You want me to buy that?" she asked Tyler. "You want me to think that you want to help Lucy out, wherever she is right now, when you didn't even treat her right when she was still alive? Are you fucking serious?"

"She's here, right now."

"What do you mean?"

"I mean, she's with us. She could talk to Emmy. She could be channeled through Cassiopeia, that woman over there. She's the reason why we figured out what happened…how Bree killed Angeline. And she's the reason why we're here right now. Because we figured that you killed Lucy."

Laurel was taken aback.

"Why are they saying that, Laurel?" Leona asked. "Are they the reason why you want to leave? Is there truth to this?"

"Mom—I—" Laurel sighed. "It's been a while, okay? And I had my reasons. And I'm your daughter, so—"

"Oh god," Leona muttered and slumped down on the floor.

Tyler turned his attention back to Laurel. "What have you got to say for yourself now, huh?"

"You're acting as if you're this goody-goody guy who loved Lucy a lot and cared for her more than anything in the world, but you know what? You never really loved her! If you did, you wouldn't have gotten together with Bree! You wouldn't have flirted with me!"

"Laurel, you know it's complicated between us."

"The only complicated thing here," Laurel shot back, "is your mind."

"But I never killed anyone."

"So, I'm seriously way too evil just because I killed someone? What are you, then? You're like, the world's cleanest person now? Aren't you insane, huh? Why would you even think that way?"

"Laurel, please. Just…"

"And why'd you even get together with Angeline? What was she? Your last choice? You wanted to marry her because what? She's nice? She resembles Lucy the most? You never loved her, either!"

"You can't say that," he said. "I loved Angeline. It was… We probably were together because it seemed convenient, but I loved her. She was someone that I loved because she was there, but that doesn't mean my feelings weren't real. I loved her with all that I could, Laurel, and she loved me, too."

"She loved you, yes, but I doubt that you actually loved her."

"We're not here to contemplate the state of my love life. We're here to get the truth out about Lucy's death."

As time goes by, you'll realize that things you once thought were important aren't actually that important; that life is more than the little details, that it is something bigger, stranger than what we believe it to be.

You cannot quantify your feelings. You can never judge someone for what he feels, or for what you think you know about him. Sometimes, what people show on the outside are merely just facades of who they really are inside.

But there are some people you can never get through to. There are some people who are just so complicated; who are responsible for making themselves complicated.

Because usually, the more complicated you are, the less people figure you out. And when people can't figure you out, you know that you're one step ahead of them, in one way or the other.

Chapter 47
I Need To Talk To Her

"What do you mean?" Tyler and Laurel were stopped in their reverie when they heard Emmy talking to an unseen force in the room: Lucy.

"Luce," Emmy continued, "I don't think that's possible."

"But I want to," Lucy said. "There are a lot of things I want to talk to her about. I could use Cassiopeia."

"It would be dangerous," Cassiopeia said. "I think I may have used all of my power already...and it's—"

"Nonsense!" Lucy said and as she said that, some of the jars displayed on a shelf in the den fell down.

"What the hell was that?!" Laurel screamed.

"Is—is this Lucy girl around?" Leona asked.

"She's been here all along," Emmy replied, then turned to Lucy again. "Luce, calm down. We can take care of this."

"No, you can't!" Lucy screamed. "That's what you've been saying all along! That you'll make things right and everything will be okay but we're still here and you still haven't gotten anything out of her except for all her denials! I WANT TO TALK TO HER!" She took a vase from the center table and threw it on the floor.

"Oh my god," Laurel cried out, horrified. "What does she want?"

"She wants to talk to you," Emmy said.

"What—"

"Okay," Cassiopeia said. "Okay, Lucy, it's okay. You can come inside me now."

"Good. I've long been ready," Lucy said and before Cassiopeia was entirely ready, she made her way inside her. Cassiopeia's eyes turned straight forward, like her soul wasn't inside her anymore. Then, she walked towards Laurel. Emmy and Libby held hands out of fear.

Lucy, in Cassiopeia's body, finally spoke. "Hello, bitch," She said to Laurel, "How would you like to start telling me about the time you had sex with Tyler right after I was buried?"

When you know others' secrets and you suddenly blurt them out aloud, you know that you'll be able to get their attention and make them your prey because there's nothing worse than having your own secrets used against you.

When you use others' secrets against them, there's almost a hundred percent chance that they'll do what you ask them to, because they know that if they don't then you'd have something to use against them.

It's not right, you know? Using people's secrets against them.

But then again, if you don't do it, then you'd be weaker than them.

The bottom line is that there comes a time in life when you have to stand up to people; when you have to use whatever it is that you have in mind to make them fall down because you've been oppressed for too long.

Sure, revenge is evil, but in this day and age, it's almost everything that you have. So, why not, right?

Chapter 48
I'm So Sorry

"Wha-what did you just say?" Laurel asked Lucy. She then turned towards Tyler. "Did you tell her?"

"What? No," Tyler said. "I never…I never told anyone about it."

"You had sex?!" Libby said. "Ew."

"You bet they did," Lucy said. "And they did it the day of my funeral." Laurel was close to crying. "I—Lucy, it wasn't—I didn't—"

"You didn't mean it?" Lucy asked and laughed. "I'm sorry, Laurel, but I don't believe you. If you didn't mean it then you probably wouldn't have killed me, right? If you were so sweet and nice and naïve, you wouldn't have done anything that you knew would hurt me. But what did you do?"

"You went and killed me like you didn't care for me at all. You pretended to be this girl who was so nice and kind, and then when things got bad, you just decided to kill me probably because you had nothing better to do. Ha! What the hell was I thinking? Why in the world did I even trust you?"

"Lucy, I'm sorry," Laurel was crying now and even Tyler was close to breaking down.

"Did you like it?" Lucy asked. "Did you like the feel of Tyler's body with your own? Did you like his kisses? How did they feel, Laurel? Because if I remember correctly, he was a really great kisser. His lips were really soft and you could just melt in them. And I can't believe I even loved him."

"Luce—" Tyler muttered.

"Don't you dare talk to me, you fucking manwhore," she said. "You weren't content with me, right? You couldn't wait. So, you had to have Bree instead. And because you weren't content with Bree, you had to flirt with Laurel, too. You're just a manwhore."

"That's not true," Tyler said. "I loved you."

"You never cried for me."

"I didn't know how to deal with my feelings," Tyler said. "I didn't know how to open up; I didn't know how to tell you how sorry I was. I didn't want to believe that it was an accident but…I didn't know who to blame. They were everything I had left—"

"And you found it convenient to just get together with Angeline?"

"It had been years," he said. "We both—we all grieved in our own ways and just because…just because I couldn't cry doesn't necessarily mean that I didn't grieve. I thought of you all the time, Lucy." The tears in his eyes were flowing now. "I thought of you all the time even though I didn't really blurt it out loud. And.. and I know that what I did was shameful. I know that you wouldn't understand but… Angeline was nice. She kept me sane. She was there when I had no one to talk to—"

"Bullshit," Laurel said. "That's what you thought of me, too, right? That's what you think about all these other girls around you. You think of us as your back-up plans just because you don't know how to go through life alone." Her voice was breaking and she went on, "You know… I was so full of guilt the day that Lucy was buried. I thought I was going to go insane but then you were there and… and I thought maybe I would be able to pay for my sins soon and that things were going to be okay and we could all move on but then… you tricked me, Ty. You played me. You made me feel loved and then you just… just went ahead and left me. You never even called me. You never even made me feel like… like I mattered. That I also mattered and—"

"Enough," Lucy said. "You can cry all you want, Laurel, but you're still alive! You're not like me who's now… dead and can't go back to this world without having to borrow another person's body. You think this is easy?" she asked. "You know what? You're fucking mental. When did you start lying to me? Was everything you showed me just a lie, huh?"

"No," Laurel said through the tears. "You have to believe me, Lucy," she said. "I liked you the best among all the girls… You were nice and easy to talk to and… and believe me when I say that I was sincere with you; that I really wanted to be your friend and I really wanted to be there for you but then… then I also always had feelings for Tyler. I thought I would outgrow them, especially when I got together with Harper but… but they were just there. I couldn't let go." She took a deep breath. "I… I was really hurt when he got together with Bree. I was hurt when he pursued her more than me because… because I didn't think that she deserved him. Bree's a bitch and… and I thought I deserved Tyler more than she did."

"And then… and then that day happened. I always had an inkling that there was something bigger, something deeper that was going on between you two and… and I didn't know how to deal with it. That day, at the tea party, I also spiked my own drink without telling anyone because I wanted to keep my goody-goody, clean, smart girl image. I guess that triggered all this anger inside so when I saw Tyler kissing you, I got so mad. I got so mad that I thought… I thought maybe I should just kill you and see what happens. I knew no one would suspect me because, well, Bree's the girl whom everyone knew had this big torch of anger for you and I knew everyone would think she had something to do with your death. I thought that it would be okay for me to just go on with my life and let her take the blame. And then when I heard that she killed Angeline—"

"Because of me," Lucy said. "I prodded her to do it."

"That's insane," Tyler said. "Why would you do that?"

"Who cares? Go on, Laurel."

Laurel took a deep breath. "When… when that happened, I thought I could finally put this all behind me and just… just forget but then… Emmy came to my doorstep and—"

"And we're all here now," Lucy said. "And I'm not content."

"Lucy, that's enough," Emmy said. "Come on—"

"No," Lucy stated. "No, it's not enough. I need her to tell me everything. I need her to tell me everything from the start."

"Lucy, I'm so sorry," Laurel said. "I'm…I'm so, so sorry, just, please—"

"I said tell me everything," Lucy repeated. "From the start."

Forgiveness should be given sincerely.

Yes, they say that we should all forgive because we're just humans and there are some things we have no control over, but that doesn't necessarily mean that we can just sit down and forget about every bad thing that the person who hurt us did.

Sometimes, you need to take control of a situation, and in order for you to take control of the situation, you have to remember the hurts and pains of the past.

I believe that the reason we often get hurt is because we don't know how to quantify the bad things that people do to us. We just forgive, without learning the lesson. And sometimes, you have to remember why they hurt you because it's the only way for you not to go through that path again.

I will forgive—of course, I will. But that will happen eventually.

For now, I'll live with the pain, because this pain will lead me to the truth.

And we all know how much I've been lied to so I deserve some honesty right now.

Maybe, after everything, I'll finally learn to say goodbye to all the hurt and go wherever it is that I need to go.

Chapter 49
He's Taken, You Know

(12 years ago)

"Did you guys already study for our math quiz later?" Laurel asked Libby, Angeline, Bree, Don, and Harper while they were walking towards the cafeteria that day. It was break time and they all needed something to eat.

"Do you still need to study for that? If I had your brains, I wouldn't anymore," Don quipped and everyone laughed. Laurel rolled her eyes.

"Hey," Libby said, "you guys excited for the school dance? Don and I are so going! Right, Don?"

"Of course. Even though school dances suck, you know," he said. "We should all just go to my house and play the newest NBA game."

"That sucks," Bree said. "Wait… all of you have dates to the dance already?"

"We don't really need dates," Laurel said.

"Tell that to the marines," Bree said and the boys laughed. "Who are you eyeing, anyway?"

"What? No one. Tyler's probably the cutest but—"

"Oh no, honey," Bree said. "He's taken."

Laurel laughed. "By whom?" she said. "He seems to be conversing with Lucy there—"

"What?" Bree turned around and saw that Lucy had just run away from Tyler. She thought that it was the perfect opportunity for her to talk to Tyler so she went up to him, her group of friends trailing behind.

"What's wrong? Did my cousin do anything?" Bree asked Tyler as they went up to him.

"Yeah, man, what happened?" Don asked. For a 12 year old, he was already big and bulky—and knew that someday, he could take over this town, too.

"Nothing," Tyler said, "Nothing at all."

"You could have lunch with us." Laurel smiled kindly.

"Yeah, we can sit together," Bree smiled, too.

***

"I can't believe you got him as a date!" Libby told Bree while they were dressing up in her room that evening for their school dance. The boys, together with Don's dad, were going to pick them up in a bit.

"Of course," Bree said, proud of herself as she puckered her lips in front of the mirror. "No one's going to be able to resist my charm, except for those stupid California boys."

"Why are you staying here again?" Laurel asked.

"What's it to you?"

"Nothing," Laurel said. "I mean, you're hanging out with us and all and you barely tell us anything about your life in California. I don't think that's fair."

"You want to know about my life? You go ask Lucy. I'm pretty sure she can tell you how hard life in California is."

"She just wasn't that popular there," Angeline butted in. "And, you know, our father left our mother and she was…wrecked. She barely spent time with us there and… and that just didn't feel right. We had to move here to forget about a lot of things and so we can all move on."

"And that's that," Bree said as she put her lip gloss inside her red, cherry-printed purse. She took a deep breath and saw Lucy wearing her pajamas, walking by the hallway. "Hey, Luce!"

Lucy then took a step back and checked what the girls were doing in Bree's room. "Hey," she said, her eyes in gloom.

"Aren't you going to the party?" Bree asked then answered herself. "Oh, wait, of course you aren't going. How on earth would anyone take you to the party, anyway?" She laughed.

"I'm studying. And I've been really tired. I'm going to my room."

"Yeah, you do that." Bree snickered and watched Lucy walk away. "She's such a loser."

"Bree," Angeline muttered.

"What? It's true."

"We live in their house."

"Whatever." Bree rolled her eyes.

"Why are you so harsh to her?" Laurel asked.

"Because she deserves it," Bree said. She then heard a car honking downstairs. "They're here!"

They all went down, leaving Lucy alone in the house.

***

Later that evening, the phone rang and since Lucy was still awake - she really couldn't sleep because she was thinking of everything she's missed - she decided to pick it up.

"Hello?"

"Hello? Lucy?"

"Laurel? Hey…"

"Hey!" Laurel shot back. "Sorry for calling this late, but uhm… Bree left her purse with me. She spiked her lemonade, I think, so… Anyway," she took a deep breath, "you okay?"

"Yeah, I'm fine," Lucy said. "See you in school. I'll just… I'll tell Bree you called."

"Oh, no, you know what? Never mind. It'll be our little secret."

"But she'll be looking for her purse."

"If she would, she'd probably be looking for it now. Consider this as a little revenge for everything she's been doing to you."

"Laurel—"

"Please," Laurel pleaded. "So, uhm, see you in school?"

"Yeah, thanks."

"Don't mention it."

What really hurts is when someone pretends to be your friend, pretends that they're always going to be there for you… and then they just end up being the ones to ruin you. And you know what? That sucks.

Because trust is already so hard to give to begin with, and yet, some people have the courage to ruin you and make you feel like you're just someone who's easily played.

I don't know. Maybe there's a vibe that some people give that makes them look and feel like weaklings to others, so these other people tend to prey on them, make them feel like they're nothing.

It's okay if people you don't know do that, because, well, you really don't know them.

But then again, you can often expect that it's your friends who have the capacity to hurt you, because they're your friends and they know you the most.

That's the tricky thing about friendships: you can never really trust anyone too much because there's always the possibility that one of them would hurt you and leave you hanging—especially when you need them the most.

Chapter 50
I'll Die Without Him

Two years later, they were at a party in Don's house. Their parents didn't really know that a big party was happening, and that alcohol was involved. That's the thing about Sky Valley: everyone pretends that it's such a perfect place when the truth is that it's dirtier than any place in the world; shrouded in mysteries, and filled with ghosts.

Laurel was looking for her friends when she saw Bree standing by the porch, drinking herself to oblivion. She went out the French doors and came up to her friend. "Bree?" She asked. "What are you doing here?"

"It's a party, I can drink."

"You're obviously way too drunk."

"I'm not."

"What's this about?"

Bree took a deep breath. "I saw Tyler talking to Jessica Jenner... I think he likes her."

"What?" Laurel asked. "You know how Tyler is. He's like, friendly with everyone."

"But I don't want him talking to her. She's a slut. She's been with almost every guy in school and..." Bree was crying now. She then held Laurel by the arms. "Laurel, I don't want him to be with anyone else."

"What do you mean? Bree, you don't own him."

"But I'll die without him!" She said. "Laurel, I can't be with anyone else. I don't want to be with anyone else. I'll die without him."

"You're just drunk."

"No… No, Laurel. You have to understand. I had this… this really rough childhood back in California and I told myself that when I get here, I'll be the best version of myself that I could be. Then I met you guys and I met Tyler and… and I thought, I was finally going to get everything. You guys have all been born rich. You're in Sky Valley, for heaven's sake. And I'm just… I'm just nothing. I just want to get what I want—"

"Life doesn't work that way, Bree. And you're young. We're all young. I'm sure in a few years—"

"No, Laurel," She said. "This is it for me. Please, just—" But before she could say anything else, she fainted right in her spot and Laurel was prompted to scream for help. From then on, she promised never to speak about her feelings for Tyler, even though it hurt through and through.

***

One afternoon when they were fifteen, they were talking about their plans for the weekend, when suddenly, Tyler asked what they were doing.

"So…weekend plans, you guys?" Tyler asked.

"Well—"

"We're going to be working on that Chemistry project," Laurel said. "Right, Harper?"

"What? But that's not due for like, 2 weeks—"

"We better start early. You're coming with us, right, Luce, Angeline?"

"What?" Lucy was evidently surprised. "Right, of course."

"Sure." Angeline smiled.

"Don and I will be out on a date." Libby said. "So, unless, you want to third wheel—"

"Why don't we see a movie?" Bree asked.

"Right, that would be fun!" Laurel said. "You guys should go see the latest

Reese Witherspoon starrer. She's so cute there! What do you think?"

"Well, yeah, why not?" Tyler said unsurely. "I mean, if Bree's free—"

"Of course, I am." Bree smiled then turned to Laurel to give her a conspiratorial wink.

***

Over the years, Laurel devoted herself to her studies. She became the top student in class and would win numerous awards for joining writing contests, math decathlons, spelling bees… you name it, she was in it. She was also part of the Student Council.

She became such a busy bee that she thought she had forgotten about her feelings for Tyler, until she would often see him and Bree together. And of course, when they got together in Junior Year, she was crushed and decided that she better forget him because she was a strong girl.

She dated Edward Richies, son of Walt Richies, owner of one of the biggest water supplying stations in Georgia, and her AP Physics classmate. He was smart, but he was a little too serious. He kept on talking about plans for college, plans for work, and plans for their life that it wasn't long before Laurel felt so suffocated that she chose to break up with him.

Soon, she dated Lincoln Walsh, this guy she met at a party in Don's house. He turned out to be Don's second cousin and while Edward was slow, Lincoln was all about being fast. He wanted to take things to the next level and Laurel wasn't ready for that. He also didn't have any plans for his life so it wasn't long before Laurel broke up with him, too. It didn't take long for him to move on, anyway. She heard that he started dating someone else three days after Laurel broke up with him.

And then there was Harper. They had always been good friends so after one afternoon of studying in her house, they talked about getting together and that was that. For what it was worth, things were great between them and Laurel actually thought that she could finally forget Tyler because of Harper but then again, life had other plans.

Or, she had other plans.

When you do things that you don't really want to do, you tend to just back away.

Sure, you may still try to do these things but there will often come a moment when you'd feel like what you're doing actually doesn't mean anything, and that you'd rather give up altogether.

There will be times when the truth—when your truth and your own reality--will come back to haunt you and make you realize that you have to stop whatever it is that you're doing right now and stick to your original plan, or go make a new plan.

And these plans could be scary because more often than not, when your truth talks to you, you'd know that you have to follow it—even though others might get hurt.

In a way, I understand Laurel.

She tried to be kind all these years but then again... we all have our weaknesses.

I just wish Tyler wasn't hers, because maybe, I would still be here.

Oh well.

Some things you can no longer change.

Chapter 51
Killer Instinct

(7 years ago)

Lucy woke up in the middle of the night. She felt so hot, she needed to wash her face. It was the alcohol, she thought. She told herself that she probably should never drink again.

She opened the door to the bathroom. She was still half-asleep. She turned on the faucet and thought that it was going to be just another normal night of washing her face. Little did she know that it was the last time she would be able to do it.

The killer was already there, watching her; watching her every step—from the time she got out of the room to the time she went inside the bathroom. The killer was ready to put her plans to life—and end Lucy's life in the process.

The killer hated her before; hated her when she realized that there was something more to her than just being Tyler's friend; that she and Tyler had a past. She hated her even more when she saw her and Tyler kiss earlier.

That was the last straw, she decided.

She had long been in love with Tyler—way before Tyler and Bree got together, way before he talked to her days before prom, way before Bree and Tyler made up again.

This was the last straw.

After all, no one would suspect her of doing this. Among all of them, she was the cleanest. She was the smartest. She was the most caring—mother hen, that's what they usually called her.

The killer was Laurel.

She even laughed at this thought. Who would even think that poor, sweet, intelligent Laurel could kill someone?

Ha! Looks can really be deceiving.

Laurel went inside the bathroom and pulled Lucy's hair.

"Wh-what are you—" Lucy wasn't able to finish what she was saying. There was a lot of water in the faucet, flowing, going through different directions. Laurel pushed Lucy's head down in the sink; pushed her so hard her face bruised; pushed her so hard she threw up.

She kept on throwing up; puke all over the floor, her head so dizzy she no longer knew what would come next.

Laurel tossed her to the toilet, pushed her head so hard that she would no longer be able to breathe; pushed her head so hard that she'd die surrounded by her own puke.

"I'm sorry, Lucy," she said, "but you deserved that. You deserved all of that."

She slowly made her way out of the bathroom, went down to go to the first floor bathroom, and flushed the gloves that she was wearing. There would be no more evidence; everyone would think that it was all just an accident.

And if all else fails, they could all blame Bree.

She was the nastiest of them all. She was the bitch—but not Laurel; never Laurel.

She went back to bed with a wicked grin on her face.

***

"Ahhh! Help! Where are all of you?! Help!" Bree's screams sliced the silence of the morning, prompting everyone to wake up.

Bree was shaking and so was Libby.

Lucy was lying on the floor, her face and hair wet, puke near the toilet and on the faucet. Lucy didn't look like a normal person anymore: her lips were dry, her hands were cold—everything about her was cold and lifeless. In short, she was no longer alive.

"Oh my god," Libby said, with tears in her eyes. "Oh my god, she's not breathing—she's---oh god no—"

"What's going on?" Laurel asked.

"I don't know," Bree answered, her hands shaking, "I was… I wanted to wash my face and pee and when I opened the door, I saw her with her head on the toilet and I… I didn't know what to do." She was crying so hard now that it scared the girls. "I wanted to get her attention and when I touched her, she fell and… Oh god what are we gonna do? We'll be in a lot of trouble." She kept crying, which prompted Angeline to hug her.

They were all crying and in a state of panic now.

"We should call the police, right?" Angeline asked. "Or 911 or—"

"Don't you get it?" Libby asked, "We'll be in trouble. I'll be in trouble! You think my parents would—oh god—this is insane. Who would do this?!"

"It's probably an accident," Laurel said, "I mean… you guys were all drunk last night and maybe she had a little too much."

"And she ended up dead," Bree stated. "She shouldn't be dead. I mean… this is just…"

"Are you sure you didn't wake up last night?" Libby asked Bree. "You're fond of taunting her. I mean, maybe you were too drunk and you decided to—"

"What? Kill her?!" Bree exclaimed. "Are you insane?!"

"I didn't say that," Libby said. "But, it's just that things between you ended up on a bad note last night and I thought that maybe—"

"Oh don't be insane, Libby," Bree argued, "You're the one who slept in the same room with her! Maybe this is your fault. Maybe you put something on her drink or led her to the bathroom and—"

"You're ridiculous! Why would I even think of doing that? I have no anger whatsoever toward Lucy, unlike you!"

"Guys, enough," Angeline said. "No one wanted this to happen."

"How sure are you of that?" Libby asked.

"Guys," Laurel said, "we can't just leave her here... Let's just call—"

"Libby?"

They were startled when they heard the voice of Libby's mother, Mrs. Amelia Kutcher.

"Oh god, oh god...we're all in trouble—" Libby stammered.

"Libby?" She called out again. "I came back early, your dad's taken a side trip to San Diego. Why the hell is this house trashed? Where are you?" She was making her way up the stairs and the girls really didn't know what to do. They were stuck in the bathroom, clinging to the last few moments of their sanity.

"Libby? Why aren't you speaking?" Amelia said as she arrived in the bathroom and opened the door wide. "What's going on—" She stopped when she saw Lucy dead on the floor. "Oh my god!" She called out. "What did you do?!"

"Mom," Libby cried, "it was—it was an accident."

"Oh, it better be," Amelia said. "I'll call 911."

***

They were never able to talk to Libby again after that morning. Her parents didn't even let her attend Lucy's wake, or her funeral. Tyler didn't want to talk to them for a while. He also didn't attend the funeral.

The police said that it was an accident—like they always do when they have no idea how to solve a case; like they always do when they're too lazy to do their job.

"Do the two of you still think that I did this?" Bree asked Angeline and Laurel the day of Lucy's funeral. They were standing on one side of the cemetery, watching Lucy's body being buried in the ground.

"Let's not talk about this anymore," Laurel said, the perfect portrait of a grieving girl in her black dress and veiled hat. "What happened already happened. Let's just let her rest in peace."

"Oh god, you actually do?" Bree asked with tears in her eyes. "You think I could kill someone?" She then looked at Angeline. "Anj? Even you?"

"Bree, let's just—"

"I can't believe you," Bree said. "I can't believe you both." She ran away, ran far away from everyone, making everyone think that she was guilty; that she had something to be scared about.

Because she ran—and running is a sign of guilt.

But Laurel? No one would think that she's guilty. No one would think that she had something to do with this. No one would think that someone as pure and intelligent as she could have something to do with her friend's death.

Laurel was safe.

Laurel was happy.

Laurel got everything she ever wanted, except that wasn't really the truth because she still got heartbroken and humiliated.

She slept with Tyler the day of Lucy's funeral. They stayed by her grave for a while then decided to go to an inn. For a while, they just stared at each other until they gave it a go and started peeling off each other's clothes. They allowed themselves to get lost in each other; they allowed the haziness of the past couple days to engulf them.

She was so full of guilt, but she couldn't talk to Tyler about what she did. She couldn't just admit that she made a grave mistake, a mistake that could ruin everything. She got lost in every kiss and every touch that she thought those would be enough to make things right; she thought those would be enough to make things better.

But of course, she was wrong.

Tyler never really talked to her again. She was treated like trash. She felt like she didn't matter. She felt like things would never be okay again. She even broke up with Harper, saying that she didn't want to see him anymore because she was still hurting over Lucy's death. He would still try to contact her in college, but she would be firm in reassuring him that nothing could change and that they really were over.

In a way, she was also punishing herself.

In a way, she wanted to be eaten up by guilt; she was already eaten up by guilt.

If only he knew.

If only everyone knew.

Guilt is one thing that you can't really explain to everyone else, simply because the feeling of being guilty is different for everyone. It's something that can haunt you for the rest of your life, especially if you don't try to stop it.

Guilt is reckless. It could envelop you, make you feel trapped, and make you feel sorry for things that you don't really have to be sorry for.

And when you start feeling guilty about things you actually have to be sorry about, you feel worse about yourself that you tend to do things that you know would hurt you, because you want to hurt yourself in hopes that it could compensate for the wrong things you did.

But the thing is, nothing will ever compensate for your mistakes—no matter how you try to escape from them, you can't run away from the truth that they'll haunt you for the rest of your life.

Chapter 52
A Tale Of Two Muderers

(Present Day)

"I'm so sorry," Laurel cried after recounting her story. "I'm really sorry. Please forgive me—"

"I will forgive you," Lucy said, "But you have to be in jail. You deserve to rot in jail."

Laurel nodded her head. "I'm sorry."

Just then, Cassiopeia started coughing. Emmy and Libby went up to her. "Are you alright?" Libby asked.

"She's... she's gone," Cassiopeia said. "I mean... she's still around but..." She looked at them, "She'll only be at peace if we bring her to jail."

"There's no problem with that."

Sara Wilson and the rest of her team appeared at the door. "Laurel Hamilton," she said, "you are under arrest for the murder of Lucy Burke."

***

"So, Miss Hamilton," Sara said while they were in the interrogation room, "can you tell us what happened the day Lucy Burke died seven years ago?"

"There was a tea party and we all spiked the tea and... and while I was walking around that afternoon, I saw Tyler kissing Lucy. I always had feelings for Tyler and I thought... well, I really wasn't thinking. My mind was already clouded up by the fact that I was so mad because I had strong feelings for him and there he was kissing Lucy... That night, I watched Lucy get out of the room she shared with Libby and... and I followed her all the way to the bathroom and shoved her face down the faucet. I wasn't contented so I did the same to the toilet bowl and... and I left her dead. I threw my gloves away and flushed them so no one would find them. I'm sorry."

"And about Bree? Does she have anything to do with this?"

"No, this was entirely my fault," Laurel declared. "I'm finally owning up to it. I...I deserve to be here."

"We'll make the necessary procedures and you can talk to your attorney anytime you want. Is there anything else we need to know?"

"No, but... can I see Bree? Even for just... just one last time?"

***

The police officers led Laurel to her cell but allowed her to make one last stop by Bree's cell. Bree was alone in there, her face full of hurt and frustration, no longer the resident mean and popular girl of the past.

They caught each other's eyes and Bree spoke, her voice breaking. "You... you killed her?"

Laurel could do nothing but nod. Soon enough, both of them we're crying.

"I'm sorry," Laurel said.

"I'm sorry, too," Bree apologized, remembering how things ended up this way for her.

***

"Can you believe this, Bree?" Angeline said. "I'm getting married!"

"Of course you are."

"But...but aren't you happy for me?"

Bree laughed. "How can I not be happy for you? You're my sister." She took the hip flask from her purse. "And this calls for a celebration."

"Oh no, I—"

"Come on, Anj, just one drink."

Angeline laughed, "Okay then," she said, took the hip flask from her sister, and drank. She drank and drank until she could no longer breathe, her mind getting cloudy, her joints stiff.

"Bree—what—"

But before she could finish her sentence, she fell down to the floor leaving Bree dumbstruck for a second.

She realized that she couldn't let people see her that way. She took the hip flask, flushed the contents down the toilet, and threw the flask in, knowing it would be submerged anyway, because she had it custom-made for the occasion.

"Sorry," she muttered, no longer feeling like herself.

Then, she decided to position herself on the floor and hold her sister, like the grieving sister she should be.

"Ahh!!!!" She screamed, mustering all the painful emotions that she could, so she could get people's attention and let them see her as a victim, too.

She didn't kill her sister, that's what she would tell them.

She didn't kill her sister.

***

She wondered how things ended up this way for Laurel, too.

She wondered if now, Lucy would finally be in peace.

She wondered if this was what was supposed to happen.

Two murderers, two old friends.

They were full of hurt; full of anguish.

They were both guilty—and for now, that's all they're ever going to be.

"Let's go now," the officers said and led Laurel to her cell where she would spend a long, long time in.

They say that the truth can set you free, and while that's true, you also can't help but think over what happened, and think about how it affected everyone. You can't help but think about the repercussions of your actions because, though you just want to go in peace, you know that others would get hurt, too.

But you know, that's life.

You don't always get what you want, but you would often get what you deserve—or something like it.

It took me this long to find peace.

I hope it won't take you forever, either.

I wish you all well.

Chapter 53
Goodbye Lucy

Emmy closed the door of their house behind her and found Lucy standing behind the door, her face almost disappearing, her body not that visible anymore. It was a long and tiring day for everyone and Emmy only hoped that seeing Lucy this way meant that she was ready to go, and that she finally found peace.

"Hey," Lucy said.

"Hey." Emmy smiled.

"Thank you," Lucy said, "for everything. I probably wouldn't be in this position without you. I want to stay for longer but... I don't think I still could. And besides, you've had enough of me already."
Emmy laughed. "Luce, come on."

"No, seriously, thank you," Lucy said. "I don't know how I'll ever be able to repay you but... I promise to stay in peace. And... and maybe, be your guardian spirit or whatever?"

Emmy smiled. "I just want you to be happy."

"And you, too." Lucy smiled. "I guess you have your own problems to deal with... and someone's waiting for you right now. I have to go."

"What? Luce—"

In just a moment, Lucy was gone.

"She finally showed herself to me." Daniel said as he got out of the kitchen with Wendy in tow. "She's... weird, I have to tell you but... but she's real."

"I told you she was." Lucy smiled at him. They met each other halfway and she gave him a peck on the lips. "What are you doing here, by the way? I thought you wouldn't be home for a couple of days—"

"I decided to cut that trip short," he said. "There are other projects, anyway, and besides..." He looked her in the eye, "I knew I needed to be here. I'm sorry I've been... I haven't really—"

"Believed that I could see ghosts?"

"It was just crazy but... I'm sorry."

"You don't have to be sorry for anything." She smiled. "I'm just glad you're here."

"Me too," he said. "I saw the news and... honey, you've been through enough. You even went to Tallulah Falls. God, if something happened to you, I wouldn't know what to do with myself. I'm so sorry. I was an idiot and there's no excuse for that. I was wrong for thinking that you're not telling the truth, so feel free to punch me anytime," he told her and went on, "and I promise, next time, I won't bail. Ghosts or no ghosts."

She laughed. "I love you," she said.

"I love you, too." He kissed her on the lips and hugged her for a bit. "Hey," he said, "I brought home Alabama's best cantaloupes... maybe we could make something out of them."

"I like the idea." She smiled. "Cantaloupe pie? Or shake?"

"Or pasta?" He quipped and she laughed.

"By the way," she said, "Audrina's inviting us over for Sunday lunch. Up for it?"

"I'm up for anything." He smiled.

"Great." She smiled back. "And cantaloupes are amazing but you know what else I missed?"

"What?"

"You and me," she said, "in bed. What do you think?"

"I thought you'd never ask."

Then he took her hand and they made their way upstairs, forgetting everything that ever hurt them in the past and promising to make a new start.

So, I'm still here.

But don't worry, I'm okay. I'm...at peace, if that's what you call this.
I guess I'll just be watching over Emmy, then.

She's helped me out a lot so I'll be here if she ever needs someone to talk to, although she probably won't see me anymore.

Gratitude is important in life.

Without gratitude, you'll just be speeding through life without any feelings whatsoever and that's not a good thing.

You need to be someone who knows how to be thankful for what you have.

You need to appreciate the people who've been there for you, especially at your worst.

And that's exactly what I'm doing now.

That's what I'll always be doing.

Chapter 54
Brunch At The Brynes

"Oh, I'm so glad you're here!" Audrina greeted as she opened the door and found Emmy and Daniel outside. They were going to have Sunday lunch at the Byrne's residence.

"Audrina, hey," Daniel greeted and gave her a peck on the cheek. "I didn't know you could hear ghosts, too."

"Oh, enough about that." Audrina laughed. "I'm glad you're here."

Emmy thought that their house looked beautiful. Fake ivies lined the Greek arches. There were roses, hydrangeas, oleanders, and mums all over the place, and there was the smell of good food coming from the kitchen.

"I made some chicken and pasta and well… some strawberry macarons. They're not great, but—"

"Don't be silly, Audrina." Emmy smiled. "Come on." She walked with Audrina hand in hand towards the dining room where her dad was waiting. "Daddy!" She greeted and hugged him.

"Oh, darling, I'm glad you're okay," Her father, Troy, said. "I was so worried about you, I thought something crazy was going to happen again. What were you thinking?"

"Dad, I just had to help someone out," Lucy said as Daniel helped her sit down. Audrina poured fresh mango juice on their glasses. "And besides," Lucy continued after sipping some juice, "it was quite an adventure and you know, at least things are in their rightful place now."

"And those girls are in jail," Audrina said. "I still couldn't believe how crazy both of them were for that Tyler guy." She took a deep breath. "Speaking of Tyler, I saw him yesterday and he said that it wouldn't be long before he leaves Sky Valley. He's probably traumatized by it all. He says he's going to New York."

"Good for him, then," Emmy said. "He also deserves his peace. I don't think staying here would be healthy for him."

"I thought so, too," Audrina replied. "Anyway, there's actually a reason why we invited you here." She smiled. "Troy?"

"Uhm..well..." Troy said.

"Dad?"

"We really didn't want to announce this over the phone so..." He then held up Audrina's hand, and Emmy and Daniel saw that she was wearing a ring studded with three, small, blue diamonds. They fit her finger perfectly and she seemed to be glowing with pride and happiness. "We're getting married!"

"Oh my god, dad!" Emmy said and stood up. She went to her father and embraced him. "Oh, I'm so happy for you guys."

"You're not...you're not mad?"

"Mad? No!" Emmy laughed. "I just want you and Audrina to be happy and if you found that happiness in each other then who am I to object?" She looked at Audrina. "And besides, at least I'd have a second mom now."

"Shut. Up," Audrina said and they all laughed. "So, you'd be my maid of honor? Please?"

Emmy smiled and held Audrina's hands. "I'd love to," she said. "Mom?"

"Emmy!"

They cracked up and enjoyed the day, the rest of their lives brimming with possibility.

You know...there is an insurmountable amount of second chances in anyone's life. Sometimes, you think that you're at the end of your rope but chances are, you're just onto something greater.

Sometimes, when you feel like no good things can happen, life is just playing you around and you'd realize that there are a lot of greater and better things that are meant for you; that you only have to wait because if you keep on pushing things through, if you keep on thinking that you need to have every-thing right away, then you'd only get second best—and you do not deserve that.

Patience is important in any facet of life.

Patience is something that not everyone has, but it's something that you should try to embody because it would allow you to enjoy every moment in your life without wanting to press the forward button each time.

I may no longer be alive, but Emmy is, and you all are.

You have all the chances that you want—you just don't realize it, but you do.

So, grab on to all those chances with both your hands.

Hold on to them.

Make sure you use them—and that you live life well.

Just live the best life you could live.

That's enough.

That's more than enough.

Epilogue

It was a blustery day and in the past couple of weeks, Emmy couldn't help but blush at the thought of her father marrying the woman he now loves: her friend, Audrina.

She remembered Audrina walking down the aisle in her gorgeous pink dress and how she held the pretty bouquet filled with lavender and myrtle, just like she was a princess. She remembered the look on her father's face while he waited for Audrina at the altar.

And she remembered how they kissed, of course.

It made her glad to see her father happy because he's been through a lot over the years. She didn't think that she'd be as calm and as at peace as she was, seeing her father get married to someone else, but then again she loved Audrina and she loved her father and she knew that it was real between them. She was happy that finally, her dad wouldn't have to spend his evenings alone, reminiscing about the past that could no longer come back. She was glad they got their happy ending.

She stood up after leaving a bouquet of fresh daisies and sunflowers on Lucy's grave. She hadn't seen her again since the day that Daniel came back but she knew that she's around. She knows, and believes, that Lucy's happy now and that she's finally at peace. She would never forget her.

Sometimes, she gets to talk to Libby, too. She's now in Las Vegas, a 180 degree turn from her quiet life in Mountain Valley. Emmy's happy that she's finally doing what she wants because she knows Libby's been cooped up for too long and that made her so unhappy.

Cassiopeia went on to take a vacation in the Maldives. The events of the past couple of weeks really took a toll on her, but she's also now hailed as one of Sky Valley's breed of new heroes—and she was extremely thankful. Emmy never fails to remind her that she really did a lot to save Lucy's spirit—and make sure that two murderers are in jail because of her help.

As for her and Daniel, there's a brand new addition to their happy ending.

"What are you thinking of?" Daniel asked as he kissed her on the forehead.

She smiled as she looked up at him. "What do you think about getting some baby supplies?"

A look of confusion crossed Daniel's face. "Baby supplies? What?" Then, he looked at Emmy's belly. He thought it grew a bit from the last time he actually looked at it. "Wait," He smiled. "Do you mean—"

"Yes." She smiled and nodded her head. "You're going to be a father!"

"Oh my god!" He said and hugged her. "Oh god." He kissed her on the forehead. "Really?"

"Yes!"

"I love you!" They kissed for quite a while, the passion and joy lingering in their lips through their bodies.

Emmy laughed. "So," she said, "shall we?"

"Yes," he said, took her hand, and together they walked towards the sunlight, their hearts full of hope.

Check Out My Other Books

Sky Valley Cozy Mystery Series

Coffee, Cupcakes & Murder #1
http://www.amazon.com/dp/B00T5HOXLQ

Beaches And Coffee #2
http://www.amazon.com/dp/B00T5HSSGW

Mayhem At The Mansion #3
http://www.amazon.com/dp/B00T6G3WO0

Murderous Coffee Crumb #4
http://www.amazon.com/dp/B00T5IVM1E

Sky Valley Cozy Mystery Box Set
http://www.amazon.com/dp/B00T5IWKD8

The Ghosts Of Sky Valley Cozy Mystery Series

The Deadly Dinner #1
http://www.amazon.com/dp/B00W3T2XII

Dangerous Teas & Treats #2
http://www.amazon.com/dp/B00W3VCIGI

Into The Unknown #3
http://www.amazon.com/dp/B00W3Y611S

The Ghosts Of Sky Valley Cozy Mystery Box Set
http://www.amazon.com/dp/B00W45X6QE

CPSIA information can be obtained
at www.ICGtesting.com
Printed in the USA
LVHW081306230819
628732LV00015B/351/P

9 781320 454520